Also by Marcelle Clements
The Dog Is Us

SIMON AND SCHUSTER

New York   London   Toronto   Sydney   Tokyo

Rock me

Marcelle Clements

SIMON AND SCHUSTER
Simon & Schuster Building
Rockefeller Center
1230 Avenue of the Americas
New York, New York 10020

SIMON AND SCHUSTER and colophon are registered trademarks of Simon & Schuster Inc.
Designed by Nina D'Amario/Levavi & Levavi
Manufactured in the United States of America

10 9 8 7 6 5 4 3 2 1

Library of Congress Cataloging in Publication Data

Clements, Marcelle.

    Rock me / Marcelle Clements.
      p. cm.
    I. Title.
    PS3553.L397R63 1988   88-28717
    813'.54 — dc19   CIP

ISBN 0-671-67095-6

(continued at the back of the book)

To Marilyn Johnson

CONTENTS

part
I

CASEY SIGHS. THE TIDE ROLLS OUT.

*   *   *

They say I'm savage, well, but what do they know? Raw talent, they like to say in the reviews. Oh, Lord, nobody knows. Me neither. What the hell is this flaming column of pain in my chest? Tell me that. Nobody knows. I don't know. Shit, I would like a drink. Is that savage? Seems sort of civilized to me, frankly.

What I'm doing on this island, I don't know either. The truth is, I came on impulse, and now will have to make up some good reason. To clean myself up, I guess, seems like the most logical choice. Though to clean myself up for what, I couldn't tell you.

I've always been up for a thrill, and it's never done me a bit of good. Now I give up. Really, I do. I know you don't believe me, but I do. The thrill-to-garbage ratio just hasn't panned out for me. I mean the garbage you have to clean up afterward, the debris of your life, to say nothing of the wreckage all around you, since there always seem to be some fools hanging around ready to come along for the ride, and they don't know how to take care of themselves any better than you do. At least in my experience, which, granted, may not be worth much. Worth shit, really, when you consider my record.

Oh golly, what a mess, what a grievous mess I left behind in New York.

I've never been very tidy, in my personal life. It's funny because I have this reputation, you know, for being in control. But I've always left sloppy trails. By now it's my specialty, I guess. The only way I know how to be.

And I don't know why, either.

14

Well, if I start to look for answers, I'll never get on with this. I mean, I have plenty of answers. The elegant analyses of several expensive shrinks. (I don't know why I'm putting them down, actually, they did me plenty of good.) Plus, if I take a little drive to the bookstore (Is there a bookstore on Kaulani? Must be.), if I take a little drive to the bookstore, I'm sure I can find any number of intelligent syntheses of this and that in the culture.

I can never decide whether identifying myself with the culture is humble or grandiose.

But, anyway, I think this is an era of sloppy trails. Yes, Lord, I've got the mean motherfucking entropy blues in the morning.

Well, too bad. Tough luck. That just seems to be the way the cookie keeps crumbling. Let me tell you, though, that I can take it. Yessir, I can. I'm going to feel better if it kills me. The blues and me, we've been friends and we've been enemies, we've known one another for a long time. They know me, but I know them, I know their tricks, and I've had it with them. Blues, you're going to lose. I intend to beat this rap, no matter what it takes.

I can do it. I mean, I'm sitting here in this room that's practically under the goddamn Pacific, all this ocean just a few feet away, all this sunshine, all this health food in the fridge, sweetness in the air, all these goddamn weird trees and flowers swaying and swaying and swaying, it's enough to even put you in a good mood in the morning. If I stay here long enough, I can tell, I'll get up in the morning with nary a thought of entropy and just concentrate on picking out a surfboard or something.

I wonder what time it is. No clocks in this house, and of course I left my watch on the plane. Don't know how many watches I've left on planes. Dozens, must be. It's an old habit of mine because I've spent so many nights sleeping on planes, drinking myself to sleep on planes, I've had this trick for years of wearing soft clothes and putting my watch and my barrettes in the seat pouch, so when I've finally had enough to drink that I can even think of sleeping I put my seat back and huddle under a few blankets and I can feel sort of like I'm in bed, but of course when they shake me awake in the morning I'm so out of it I usually forget everything I've put in the pouch. Unfortunately, this particular watch was a goddamn Cartier and a present from Anthony, but who asked him to get me ridiculous Cartier watches anyway?

Yes, I think that's it for me and Anthony. Talk about sloppy trails, anyway. But I have to tell you that, in my opinion at least, it's really not my fault. I mean, he broke our compact. Here I thought finally I could have a nice peaceful thing with someone. Just a few nights a week, you know, no big deal, a really good friend I'd sleep with sometimes but who wouldn't get under my skin or anything, and Anthony, who's just about as elegant a customer as I've encountered, seemed like just the ticket. Sex wasn't all that great but I've sort of had it with sex lately anyway. No, I just wanted filler material, someone to take up the available space so I wouldn't get involved with someone else. I wanted something nice and quiet so I could bide my time. Bide my time for what, I can't tell you.

Goddamn, I'd like a drink.

Well, no, none of that.

CASEY ——— DRIES OUT ON PACIFIC ISLAND.

Wish I could stop thinking in headlines.

There's no alcohol in this house, anyway, you can bet on that. Have to admit I checked when I got in last night. There's all this squirrel food in the cupboards. There are these huge vats of tropical juice in the refrigerator. Oh man what the hell am I doing in this absurd place with these grotesque vats of pineapple-papaya juice in the refrigerator, staring at this goddamn ocean that means nothing to me. Nothing. Nothing. Fucking stupid ocean.

Wonder what time it is. Michael said he'd call in the morning. It's the morning, I know that. The sun is low. Even I know the sun's low in the morning.

Maybe it's the late afternoon?

No, I think it's the morning, because of the light. I could turn on the radio, but if there's anything I don't want to hear, it's music. No music, thank you. I've had enough, don't ask me. No thanks.

16

When Michael called and told me everything was all set for this house he asked if I wanted a piano in it and I said no. You can always borrow one of my guitars, he said, if the spirit moves you. I hope that dumb-ass spirit stays wherever it's hiding, I said, I don't want to see his ugly face. And he laughed and said he knew what I meant, which I guess he does.

When I got off the plane last night, Michael and Leslie were there, with these leis, you know, these garlands of flowers, which I thought was sweet, actually, since I'd never known Michael to do anything so hokey, but when I looked at Leslie's face I saw she was sweet in that way, a sweet, pure face with almost nothing written on it, so I understood how Michael had gotten to this, standing in a balmy night with these flowers in his arms. It was weird. The whole thing was weird, to tell you the truth. For instance, Michael kissed me on the cheek, and I suddenly flashed on the fact that the last time Michael kissed me was in front of 55,000 people. No kidding. It was his last night with the band, though I didn't know it at the time. I used to do this thing on stage then, when I'd walk over to one of the guys and sort of dance around him a little, and that night when I got close enough to Michael to see his eyes I noticed he looked real strange. His pupils were huge, which was odd, you know, under the lights. Everyone's pupils are usually unbelievably contracted under those ridiculous lights. So I remember thinking, What the fuck is he on tonight? and then he grabbed my hair and pulled my face close and kissed me on the mouth for a real long time and the crowd was howling, howling. The band just vamped for a while, and then I pulled away, which I guess maybe I wouldn't have done if I'd known he was kissing me goodbye.

I didn't even look for him after the set. Went to my dressing room for a drink and a Librium and then I really can't remember what I thought that night or whether I wondered why he'd done that, though I remember I was in bed with the guy who was playing keyboards at the time and I thought of Michael's kissing me on stage. The next day Ken called me and said we'd have to find someone else for the rest of the gig because Michael had checked out. What do you mean, checked out? I asked Ken, and for a minute I had this horrible icy blackness in my chest because I thought he was dead, but no, Ken said, when he rang his room to wake him up the hotel operator told him Michael had checked out during the night and had said to say he was sorry.

And that was it. Sorry. After ten years. I told the keyboards guy to go back to his own room so I could think. But I couldn't think. I don't remember what my brain did. I know I didn't cry. Those years, I never cried.

Never, never, never gonna cry over you. Never gonna cry over you, baby.

Wish I could stop thinking in cheap hook lines.

Wish I could stop thinking. It's not even thinking, sometimes it seems to me. I mean there's one or two main threads, but then there are these scores and swarms of hordes of I don't even know what to call them. It's like armies of ants. Battalions of ants marching hither and thither in the passages of my brain. I can't tell if it's hundreds or thousands. Maybe it's electrical impulses. They say all thoughts are electrical impulses. Maybe it's hundreds of thousands of ants.

Well, man, it's kind of early to be thinking of battalions of ants, isn't it?

Maybe the reason I'm anxious is that I'm thinking about Michael in a way that may not be so good. Fact is, everything was over between us so long ago, I mean really, really long ago, way before that time he kissed me on stage. So I'm kind of surprised I have these sort of strange feelings. This is not a good time to make trouble, Casey. No, I'm sick of making trouble, honest I am. And the guy's cleaned himself up. Shit, the guy's survived, which is amazing in and of itself at the rate he was going, and his girlfriend is pregnant and this is no time to make trouble. And actually, I don't even know why I'm even thinking of this at all, even one little bit, because never mind Michael and his pregnant girlfriend, *I* can't afford any more trouble, not even one little bit.

Let me tell you, it's positively astonishing how much I would like a drink. I mean, like even a glass of wine or something. Isn't

18

it absolutely amazing how much a human being can desire a drink?

Well, let's take it easy here. I mean, these situations with old lovers are always something of a turn-on. I mean, anyone or anything you can't have is a turn-on, right? even if you're the one who's decided you don't want it. Besides, you don't have to act out all the garbage in your brain, as all my old shrinks used to say.

Maybe that's the problem of doing what I do: you do violence to yourself over and over again to act out on stage and then you don't know how to stop it anymore.

In a way, the weirdest thing about having these thoughts in the first place is it's been such a long time since I've thought about a man this way at all.

Well, I can keep a lid on it. I got a job to do here, man. I've got to straighten up and fly right. I've got to get myself together. Though, to tell you the truth, I don't even know what myself is anymore. Maybe myself is scattered in a zillion little pieces on a thousand stages, in thousands of beds in motel rooms, in a thousand empty bottles.

Come on, let's not get carried away. A thousand empty bottles? I must be kidding. I can't believe how weepy I am. I can't believe this has happened to me, really, sitting here in this maudlin heap at the end of the aimless road on this nowhere island. Though, let's face it, my road was ended everywhere. That's why I'm here.

After all, what the hell was I going to do with myself in New York? Tell me that. What is the way out of this for me? I can't go for the aging rock star gig, I really can't. The grand bourgeois lifestyle, the oldies on stage, no, fuck that. That's not me. No, the first half of my life was too exciting for me to make do now with leftovers. No. I don't know, I'll have to think of something. I mean, at least I've got some equipment, maybe I'll think of something. Or maybe I won't think of anything but find some way to transform it into something else. Or maybe I have to resign myself to what I am and the time I live in, which is undoubtedly the bitterest pill of all. My fate, in other words. Thanks a lot. Bitter as bile. Bitter and heartbreaking as the blues.

But then, when has there ever been a blues singer who wasn't heartbroken?

And, anyway, who's to say I won't get better here? Michael, after all, was a much bigger wreck than I ever was. I mean, Michael's habit was no kidding around. Michael had a habit on his habit. And he was weaker than me, too. Truth is, that's part of why I could never go for him all the way, I mean if I'm really completely honest, I always knew he was weak somewhere and that I was stronger. Though maybe that's genetic. Or maybe I just had more to live for, too. Or thought I did.

Hell, if Michael can straighten himself out here I don't see why I can't. Of course it did take him several years. I don't have several years. I mean, to do what I do. In several years I'll be over forty, which is like saying in several years I'll have fallen over the edge of the universe.

Or, more precisely, to do what I did.

Shit. I'm doing a rapid sink here. A dive. A deadly descent into the yawning pit. Maybe I should get dressed. This is like too hellishly stupid sitting here in my nightgown staring at this ocean, wishing I had a drink. I don't know what to wear. I don't think I brought the right stuff. I packed in such a hurry with Anthony standing there pissed off lecturing me about what an idiot I was to be going. Of course I have to admit it wasn't so nice of me not to let him know until the night before. But in a way I was right, I mean something told me he'd behave like an asshole, and he did. He couldn't stand to lose: he thought he was going to be the one who'd make me get better. They all think that. They all think that and then they hate you when they fail. Or when I fail. Or whatever. Of course that doesn't alter the fact that I was a bit of a cunt, actually. I mean, Anthony was there when I ran into Michael. It was one of my better nights and I was reading the paper and saw there was this saxophone player I really love, Eddie Lockjaw Davis, playing at the Blue Note, and I said, Hey, let's go, and Anthony said okay, and then right when we walked into the Blue Note I saw Michael sitting there by himself at a table in the back corner just like he always used to and I stopped so short Anthony ran into me.

Or I should say—I'll tell you, it was strange, because at first I didn't realize it was Michael, I just hadn't seen him in such a long time. For part of a second, what I saw was this great-looking guy sitting at a table in the back, before my brain worked out the information that it was Michael. Then I was so surprised it was Michael that I forgot the shock I had just from registering a really attractive man, which is something I hardly ever do anymore, though I can't tell you for sure whether it's because I don't care anymore or because I hardly ever see a man my age I think is great-looking. It's ridiculous but I'd forgotten how much I love the way Michael looks. It's always been a big item in how his personality wound up being configured because he was so beautiful it used to create a kind of shield between him and other people. Like it was really difficult for people, especially people who didn't know him well, to penetrate that, to go beyond just the way he looked. Well, but so that night at the Blue Note, I decided immediately he still looked really cool, I have to say. Maybe not quite as sort of pure-looking, just because he's older, and there's more written on him, but in a way that's cooler. Plus, I guess if I'd thought about it I might have assumed he wouldn't look so hot considering what he's been through. I mean that he'd be really wasted and devastated-looking. But he looked real healthy, actually, tanned so his eyes seemed even bluer, and his face still real sculpted-looking, and the way he leaned back in his chair looking super-loose but then when you get close you realize how tense his body is and that he's always tapping his foot or something, just seemed as incredibly cool as ever. Star quality, definitely. From when we were kids, right from the start, Michael always looked fantastic in every single publicity shot we ever had made of the band. The other guys used to make jokes about it when we'd be going through contact sheets and everyone including me looked real wormy in ninety percent of them and Michael always looked perfect. It embarrassed him.

Well, so then I walked over to the table and said hi and I could tell it was weird for Michael too. I mean, the whole thing was weird. It was nice, though. I mean, it's odd but there were no hard feelings, too much time had gone by. He said he was in town just for the night, had been to visit his parents and was recuperating in Manhattan for the night before going back and I thought that was just like him to decide to recuperate by going to listen to Eddie Davis and I remembered how much I always liked Michael, I mean what a good friend he always was, in the old days. So when he asked how I was doing instead of answering this and that the way I usually do, I said I'm pretty burned out, I guess, and he looked at me and I could tell he knew I really was far gone in some way, and he said, Maybe you should come to Hawaii, to Kaulani. A place, he said, that's full of burnouts who got themselves together. No kidding, I said, really? And he said, Yeah, chock-full. Michael's the most consistently ironic person I've ever known. That was always part of his appeal, that even if you knew him well you never knew when he was kidding and when he was for real. A great place to get your spirit together, he said. So then I knew he was being ironic but I noticed Anthony looking prudently blank. A beautiful place with a real healing vibe, said Michael. And then Anthony laughed because he'd finally gotten it. Anthony is so fucking cautious, socially. I don't know. Maybe that's not fair. I used to think of it as tact. I used to think Anthony had the most astonishing tact and discretion. Maybe he does. I can't tell anymore what's true from what's distorted. When will this tantrum be over, for Pete's sake?

Anyway, then the band came on and we couldn't talk anymore, but as I sat there thinking I swear that's when I decided to do it, after just one minute's conversation, I thought, Why not? Just do it, just do it. I don't know what it was. Maybe I'd had exactly the right amount of scotch. Maybe it was Eddie Davis' playing, which has always sent me, you know. I don't know what it is. Sometimes I think the blues, especially played on a saxophone or sung by a certain kind of voice, a black voice, sweet and raunchy, which is the way Eddie plays, well sometimes I think that kind of music has psychopharmacological properties. Yeah, well, the blues have been making depressed people feel better for a long, long time. Anway, I was feeling a little better, I guess. Tip-off is, it had been ages since I'd even

22

gone to hear any music. I was feeling a little better and I suddenly thought BAIL OUT. You know what I mean? When you like see this tiny little door you can crawl through and maybe you're going to save yourself? And another part of my mind was reminding me I hadn't even seen Michael in years and who knew what kind of an asshole he might have turned into and who knew what kind of an asshole his wife might be and in fact the odds were real terrific that this place, Kaulani, might be full of assholes and I'd be freaking out on this inane island on the other side of the world that was full of assholes. To say nothing of the little problem of Anthony and my apartment and my goddamn manager who I knew was going to absolutely go through the roof. And all those people waiting for me to go into the studio. And the frigging tour planned. And the whole horrendous operation that depends on me. And the whole thing. And everything. But I just thought, Do it. Just do it. Then after the set we talked for a while and Michael actually suggested to me in a serious way that if I wanted to come he'd help me arrange it and I saw he could see I was in trouble and that he was still my friend, after all these years, that he'd help me. How long has it been? More than a decade. It's funny, what a long time it had been since I'd felt I really had a friend. So then I said I just might do that. And both Michael and Anthony smiled. And I'll tell you something weird that was the thing that conclusively convinced me: Anthony smiled because he thought it was preposterous, I mean he thought I'd never take off to some silly island just because someone I hadn't even seen in years suggested it. But Michael remembered all the times long ago when I'd say I just might do it and then we'd hitchhike to California or pop a pill of unknown substance or whatever. So that made me feel like my old self a little, you know, when I wasn't so brain dead, when I wasn't so deadly tired all the time and deadly wasted hopeless.

An island full of burnouts, for God's sake. So I asked myself, Am I burned out yet? Well, just about, brothers and sisters. Not quite, but I'm getting there. The truth is I'm exhausted from trying to appear as if I'm together. Bail out, I thought. Get on the plane. The time has come to cool out somewhere and try to figure out what the real options are instead of dragging my ass through my life. Plus, I must admit, this constant tippling has gone too far. I mean, my face, to tell you the truth, is really starting to look like shit. That's all I need. I looked at myself in the mirror the other day and found myself wondering if I couldn't use an old photo for the album cover. And it's not the question of the goddamn album cover, you understand, but just that I don't want to feel that way. No, no, none of that for me. Yet. Not yet, okay? I don't want to feel like an old ridiculous lounge lizard yet. I mean, turning into an aging, decaying, boozy bluesy white chantoozie would be like just too pat, you know, just too fucking corny for words. I'm not ready yet to turn into a caricature of myself. Give me another minute to see if I have anything left. Hey, it's not just anybody who can do what I've done so far. And, man, I've bled for it, you know? I've already earned one hot minute for myself, let me have a chance at one more.

Well, yeah, so here I am. Ivy divy. What next? Sitting here in my goddamn nightgown waiting for the phone to ring like when I was little and used to wake up before anyone else in the house and every minute was three centuries. Why can't I just go back to sleep? Why can't I sleep anymore? I'm going crazy.

Maybe I'll put on a bathing suit and check out this absurd unreal blue ocean. This ocean annoys me already. I mean the sound, man, does not stop.

I hadn't thought in ages about that day on Martha's Vineyard with Michael and Nick.

Hey, none of that. Push it away. Set up a holler in your brain that's louder. I can yell louder than the sea, any day.

Okay, where was I? Bathing suit. Beach. Yes, sir, I can tell this fucking massive blue puddle and me are going to do some heavy tangling with one another.

* * *

24

When Michael and Leslie pull into the driveway, they see Casey standing on the beach beyond the house, looking out, fists on her hips. They both call out but Casey doesn't hear, so it isn't until they're standing next to her at the edge of the ocean that they enter her field of vision and she starts.

"Sorry," they say simultaneously.

Casey puts her hand on her chest. "Oh, Jesus. I'm not nervous or anything . . ."

"Yeah," says Michael. "Well, it'll take you a while before you mellow out and get blissed out like the rest of the crowd around here."

"Yeah, sure, fat chance," says Casey.

"You'd be surprised," says Leslie.

Casey studies Leslie's face for a moment to try to measure her degree of irony, but can't tell. Leslie's face is hard to read, deeply tanned like a surfer's. Her hair is flaxen and straight. "You sure are pretty," Casey says to Leslie.

Leslie smiles and looks down and gestures at her abdomen. "I'm pretty pregnant," she says.

"Pregnant is pretty," says Michael.

"And you have fantastic eyes," says Casey. "I've never seen eyes like yours."

"It's from all these years Leslie's spent looking at the sea," says Michael. "That's my theory. When you have a minute, I'll explain the physics of it to you."

"Michael's got lots of theories," says Leslie.

"Yeah," says Casey. "He always did."

"Sorry we came by so late," says Leslie. "It was pretty gnarly around our house this morning. Sebastian lost his truck."

"How old is Sebastian?" asks Casey.

"Four," says Leslie. "But he's going through some weird phase. When he can't find any of his stuff he completely freaks out."

"Yeah, the last couple of weeks, he's had a hellhound on his trail," says Michael.

Casey laughs. "Well, in that case, I'm sure he and I will get along splendidly."

"Do you think you want to come and have dinner with us tonight?" asks Leslie.

"Sure," says Casey. "That would be nice. But I don't want you to feel I have to be around all the time, you know. I mean, you don't have to feel obligated to watch me all the time or anything."

"We won't. But it's nice that you're here," says Michael. "I'm glad you're here."

"Me too," says Leslie. "I've heard all these stories for years, you know. Although, even before I met Michael I always really liked your music."

"Mm," says Casey. "Thanks."

"Have you had breakfast?" Michael asks.

"No, but I'm not too hungry. Jet lag, you know. Do you want to go in and have some juice?" she says. "I think that's about all there is in the fridge right now."

She picks up her own glass, stuck in the sand beside her.

"I can't believe I'm drinking juice in the fucking morning," she says. "I'm sure it's going to disrupt my digestive process."

"You'd be amazed how many disgustingly healthy habits you can pick up around here," says Michael.

"I'll have to pick up some Pepsi," says Casey. "Got to have at least one Pepsi in the morning. I mean, there are limits."

"Why don't we go shopping?" says Leslie.

"Or do you want to just go for a drive to look around first?" asks Michael.

"Uh, whatever," says Casey. "I'm easy."

They start walking toward the house. Casey turns as they reach the screen door.

"Pretty fantastic," she says, gesturing toward the sea.

"Perfect waves," says Leslie. "Kona wind."

"The fucking winds have names!" says Casey. "That's great."

"We've been having a kona wind for a few days," says Leslie. "It'll stick around until the trade wind comes and chases it off."

"How can you tell," says Casey, "which wind it is?"

"Well, you can always look at which side of the sail the windsurfers are on," says Leslie. "I'll show you when they come out in the afternoon."

"It's pretty interesting, actually," says Michael. "There are all these old myths too, about each of the winds. Leslie knows all this stuff. She's been here for ages."

"How long have you been here?" Casey asks Leslie.

"Since I got out of school," says Leslie.

"Where'd you go to school?" Casey asks.

"Scripps, in La Jolla," says Leslie. "Oceanography and marine biology."

"You're kidding," says Casey.

Leslie laughs. "No," she says.

"And did you become a practicing oceanographer?" asks Casey.

"No," says Leslie. "I just kind of flaked out after school. I was sick of California and decided to check out this place and then I just kind of never left. I just became your basic water lover."

"She mellowed out and got blissed out," says Michael.

"So you know all about the ocean and the winds?" says Casey. "Gee, I don't know shit about any of this stuff. I wish I knew the names of winds."

"Leslie can tell you if you want," says Michael. "Then, when you wake up every day you can look out and you'll know why the waves have a certain height or the ocean's a certain color and what spirit is blowing that morning."

"Well," says Casey, "I certainly could use something new to mull over in the morning."

"Have you been up long?" asks Leslie as they walk into the house.

"No," says Casey. "I just got up, just before you came. Slept great."

*　　*　　*

Am I going to be able to take it here? Jesus, talk about no action. Can I really hang out in a place with no sidewalks? I bet there isn't a single bar on this island. All this fucking serenity they talk about just gives me the willies, if you want to know the truth. What am I doing here? No, man, really, I don't believe I have the temperament for this shit.

Though what is my temperament? I'd like to know.

I wonder how big a mistake it was to walk out on Anthony. Well, but I didn't strictly walk. Any time I want, I can call and ask him to meet me here. That's all it'll take for both of us to be able to pretend that nothing really insulting happened, that I didn't really walk out on him.

At least, I think so. Or has Anthony just been waiting for me to walk out on him? I don't know. He's so clever, I don't really know what he's thinking. That's what gets me every time; he's truly clever. I can't decipher him, he's too smart and too complicated. In fact, it's been a real long time since anyone's kept me on my toes as adeptly as Anthony does.

In a way, lately, it's all that's kept me going. I mean, kept my mind off the streets, kept me from tumbling conclusively over the ever-present edge. I should be grateful to him. Why aren't I grateful?

Anyway and sometimes I wonder, about Anthony, whether *he* isn't the one amusing himself with *me*. . . .

Oh, man, it's too tough for me. I'm so tired. I just want to be left alone. Just leave me alone, okay?

*   *   *

"Just let me know if you want to be alone," says Michael. "All right?"

"Don't worry, I'll let you know," says Casey. "What are you guys doing tonight?"

*   *   *

Well, so I've actually taken up running. Can't believe it's come to that. After all these years of holding out about this physical stuff. Of course, I could afford to, I just have the kind of body that takes abuse like a trouper, but if I don't do something with myself I'll just sit around the house wishing I could have a drink, which is not my idea of a good time. Neither is this, but so what if I engage in just one more cliché in the culture? I mean, I am a cliché in the culture. So, you know, so what?

I sort of feel like a jerk, I can tell you, but the fact is there's no one to see me. Except for the unseen audience, by which I guess I only mean myself of course but I'd feel like a jerk whether I was running or not so I might as well feel like a jerk and get healthy. I mean, I'm assuming I'll get healthy if I keep going with all this stuff. Anyway, I have to admit it makes me feel better. I run along the paths in these sugarcane fields, and it's sort of dreamy. I tried running on the beach in front of the house but it's too tough on the legs and, anyway, the ocean is too distracting.

So I drive here, to the cane fields, and park off the side of the road. Red dirt paths, miles and miles of them. There's red dirt all over my running shoes and my socks. It's a color I've never seen anywhere else, this red. Nor, I guess, the blue of this particular sky, unrelentingly placid. The sun is something fierce. Even though I only run early or late in the day, I start sweating like a devil almost immediately. Which feels kind of good, in a way. The cane is as tall as I am, taller, so I run in a kind of tunnel, a very silent tunnel. I make a thumping noise, running. Sometimes I sing a little to the beat. Can't help it. But it's not so bad, so I run and sweat and sing. Running's hard, but in a way it makes me feel better to have another pain to distract me.

It's hard. Today seems particularly hard, I think. Maybe the novelty's worn off already. Got to keep going though. I've become like a fucking cop with myself. Twenty minutes minimum.

Fifteen to go.

I still feel pretty crummy. Let's put it this way: I feel horrible. But I have moments of feeling a little better, which, in the last few months in New York wasn't happening at all, except for, you know, those few moments, when you're drinking, when you're at exactly the right point. The trouble with alcohol, though, is that you only feel all right for very few moments. All the rest of the time, when you're drinking, you've either not drunk enough, or drunk too much. Just that tiny bit of respite. Even if it makes you feel worse afterward. I mean, what is it: worse than worse. There's a point when you're feeling so bad that worse is just an abstraction, a moot point.

Anyway, so I haven't been drinking, except for a little wine at dinner. I bought a bottle of scotch but it just sits there on the counter. Michael drinks a little wine too. Leslie doesn't drink at all, because she's pregnant, though she still smokes dope, which I have to say I find incredible. She's convinced it's okay to smoke while you're pregnant and for all I know she's right. It's not what I find incredible anyway, but that her mind's steady enough she's not afraid of rocking it. But I'm projecting, of course. I mean, let's face it, that's why I drink, is to steady myself. The rocky rocker, that's me. But then it seems to me Leslie's pretty steady. Amazing steady, as a matter of fact.

I like Leslie. I think I like Leslie more and more. She's smart though she's one of these people who don't need to show they're smart. Unlike me, let's face it. But then I've always been a show-off, haven't I? Plus maybe I became defensive at some point since everyone always assumes that if you're a rock 'n' roll musician you must be submoronic.

I don't know. Maybe they're right, now that I think of it. Can't say I've lived very intelligently or anything.

Anyway, Leslie is also so goddamn contained. That's why she can smoke, I think. She's truly, truly calm. I actually don't think I've ever known close-up anyone who is like that. I used to see people who seemed like that, but I always assumed it was bullshit. I mean, among the people I've known, I think it was bullshit. They'd act cool and everything, but they were actually these sniveling wrecks inside. But Leslie is, as she would put it, really together.

Free, I guess, in a certain way. But is that possible? I don't understand people Leslie's age. Someone like Leslie can take advantage of everything we got without paying for it the way we did. Oh, I don't know. Maybe Leslie would have been herself at any time. I can't figure any of that out anymore.

But Leslie's sort of a lesson for me, actually. Because she's so small and pretty and talks like a hippie and all, if I'd met her under other circumstances, I'd probably dismiss her. But she's sly, and delicate. For instance, I don't really think I intimidate her. She's wrapped her mind around who I am and managed to separate that from who I'm supposed to be better than 99 percent of those supposedly sophisticated creeps in Los Angeles or New York, that's for sure. Christ, these people, they drive me crazy. They've met a few famous people, so they think they're hip, they transcend celebrity. So I meet these people I've never seen before in my whole goddamn entire life, okay, and they act like they *know* me. That's their way of being cool. I mean they spend like three minutes with me and they haven't got a clue as to who or what I am and they think that because they've heard my songs or seen my face in the papers they can behave as if they were with their old college roommate.

What am I so pissed off about, anyway?

I haven't had sex in ages. Not in ages. Though you might say other people have had sex with me. I haven't played the piano, for my own pleasure, in months, if not years. I can't remember when I last ate something delicious.

Sometimes I wonder what it would be like to go and get plastic surgery and not ever be recognized again. Well, of course, the truth is I wouldn't like it, don't think I don't know that. But, still, can you imagine the peace? I can't even imagine it anymore. I think for the last ten years, at least ten years, I never go anywhere without being hit on. One way or another.

At least in the States. I can't believe how much easier it is here. The other day I was with Leslie and we ran into some friends of hers and they didn't say anything but I saw from their expressions they knew very well who I was and Leslie must have sensed me stiffening because she immediately said See you later, and gave me an out.

I bet Leslie protects Michael all the time, one way or another. Leslie understands a lot of things. But maybe it's also because she's got a maternal thing, too, which is pretty funny. I mean, I can't stop thinking it's funny, and once in a while I just laugh out loud when Leslie delivers one of these really ingenuous lines about getting rid of toxicity in the ocean and so forth. Sort of a maternal New Age teenybopper, but she's got too much intelligence and charm to seem like a parody. But then she's young. Thirty.

I was already a wreck at thirty. I don't know. Have I ever not been a wreck?

God, it's hot today. Ten minutes to go.

I just want to get back to Birmingham
I just want to get back to Birmingham
I got a gang in Third Alley
don't know where I am

Come to think of it, Michael, in his own way, is pretty maternal too. I can't believe how he gets along with Leslie's kid. I never could have imagined him so protective. In his own cool way, I mean. That little boy adores him. That little Sebastian, he's a real live wire already. He's got some powerful combination of poetry and wildness. And those eyes . . . That kid is going to be a real killer. Wouldn't want to break his heart yet.

Michael is still cool, it's funny. But he's got this sort of sweet quality back that he used to have and then lost for a long time. It's not just that he's cleaned himself up, it's as though he's kind

34

of *located* himself, in a way. I don't know what he had to do to get there. I don't even want to think about it. He certainly was the worst off of all of us. That is, all of us who didn't die. He was real bad off. He was utterly wasted.

Maybe he did die, in a way. Sometimes it makes me sad to see him like this. Which, I mean, is ridiculous. But I can see how he did it: he just accepted getting by with small expectations. By giving up, in a way. Though giving up what, I can't tell you. Anyway, I guess that kind of humility scares me.

Sometimes I find myself staring at his hands. He's got real beautiful hands. They look like a musician's hands. It's funny, because the very farthest back I can remember Michael is—I guess we must have been around sixteen or seventeen then, sitting on the bed with a Byrds record on his KLH, and Michael would play along on the guitar and he had a kid's hands, I realize now, but also, his nails were bitten down so low it was really far out. I mean, they always used to be a little bloody. It was horrifying to look at. He was good, too, he was already really good on the guitar, but there was something sort of heartbreaking about it, because of the way his nails looked.

He used to play with his eyes closed, so sometimes I looked at his face, sometimes I looked at his hands. Then when the record was over, he'd lean back against the wall and open his eyes and say in that nasal voice he had that was a joke but you'd forget it was a joke because he always used it, he'd say, "So, Casey, do you think I'll be a star?"

He used to do great imitations too. Like he had this fantastic Chuck Berry imitation that he used to do that was incredibly funny. He stopped all that when we went on the road. I think I only heard him do his Chuck Berry imitation one more time, that night Nick flipped out.

* * *

"Will you marry me?" Sebastian asks Casey.

"You don't want to marry me," says Casey.

Sebastian drops his pail and shovel in the sand, and rolls over on Casey.

"Hey!" says Casey.

Sebastian lies still on Casey's belly, his head on her breast. "I am like a little fish," he says, "and you are the biggest of all the fishes and I wish I could swim inside of you."

"Well," says Casey. "Gee."

"Sebastian," says Michael. "Do you want to go into the ocean for a swim?"

"No," says Sebastian.

*　　*　　*

God, I hadn't thought of that night in years. I don't even remember exactly when or where it was. Maybe it was Chicago. Yeah, I think it was at the ——— Hotel. Some time in the late sixties or early seventies it must have been, because it was still Michael and Nick and Will and Smitty, and Ken was still traveling with us. Well, yes, we were all there, so it must have been the first tour. But I'm not sure whether it was early or late in the tour. On the other hand, I was already singing "Forget the Rest," so we already had a hit.

It was Chicago, I just remembered we were all supposed to go hear some blues when we got through. Those days I used to not want to go anywhere where I had to sit still after the show because I was always too wired, but the boys really wanted to check out these Chicago dudes. I can almost remember who was playing. I'll remember in a minute. Anyway, the guys were totally flipped about the prospect of these blues legends in the actual flesh and they talked me into going too, and I'd said okay but they had to come back to the hotel with me first so I could change, because I didn't want to be by myself.

We went back in several cars, I was in a car with Ken and Will. I remember, in the car they were talking about the gate and the grosses, which really annoyed me. It wasn't so surprising from Ken, who was our manager and who never talked about anything except grosses, takes and royalties. But from Will, I thought it was really too much. Will had been in the band almost from the start. From the start, really, because before he joined us Michael and Nick and I were basically just fooling around. But

Will had been in another band, I mean he left this other band that actually had gigs in clubs around New York and everything, which was a big deal at the time because you have to remember that in the sixties there were thousands of kids' bands around New York and most of them didn't do anything except play in suburban garages until the kids got old enough to go to college and become accountants and doctors and whatnot. Anyway, Will left this going proposition to join us and I guess it's from that point on that we started to get pretty serious about it. Will played the guitar too, but he let Michael have it and became the piano player. Practiced like a maniac, too. Everybody practiced like crazy. I started practicing singing in what I thought was a serious way. I used to sit there playing Aretha Franklin records and singing along, trying to do the turns and leaps and everything. Shit, I must have done that like hours a day for months and months. Actually, it really sort of wiped my voice out and gave me this kind of hoarse quality that everybody loved but that was just me fucking up my voice, though I didn't know it for years. Of course, I finally faced the fact I'd never sing like Aretha. Didn't have the pipes or the class or anything. But I didn't sing like anyone else either, by the time I got through. I certainly didn't sing like a white girl. That's a triumph of sorts. I guess. Anyway, at the time, I figured I'd better get good at singing because when Will started playing piano, I stopped. It's funny, when you think about it, how differently everything might have come out if a few details had been different. Anyway, I stopped playing the piano and started just singing. We all sang, I wasn't the lead singer or anything, but, by default I was fronting the group, and I used to have one or two songs to sing by myself. At the beginning, it was just one or two songs at the end of the set. It was weird to stand there and have nothing to do so I carried a tambourine, just like all the other dumb chicks. Sometimes I can't even believe it. I mean, we were ridiculous.

I don't know. Maybe we weren't ridiculous. Maybe we were sort of cute, I guess.

Anyway, Nick played bass. And we ran through a whole

bunch of drummers who were all truly lousy until we hooked up with Smitty. Smitty really bailed us out. That's when we got our sound, such as it was at the time, going. Smitty already had a truly mean beat. Plus, we were actually quite pleased to have a black drummer, which at the time was unusual. The local music scene was just about totally segregated then, by color and by class, just like in your parents' living room. So we thought that was pretty cool, despite Ken's assurances that we would have trouble on tour, which, by the way, we did, as it turned out.

Ken is Will's cousin, and he became our manager when Will joined us though at the time there wasn't much to manage. I know Ken is convinced he created the band. Maybe he's right for all I know. But he certainly was a drag. We couldn't even believe it at the time, how hyper this guy was. It seemed especially so at the time because everyone was smoking grass like crazy and it was like the most laid-back kind of atmosphere imaginable. Michael and Nick and I got together and wondered whether it was even worth it having Will in the band if it meant having this totally uncool hyper guy as manager. I don't think we ever even decided yes or no. It was just like us in those days, we didn't decide anything, and events would just sort of unfurl on their own.

Ken thought we should decide everything in a logical businesslike way, and I guess he thought taking Smitty on was a bad business decision, which just goes to show you how these business people can make horrible business decisions, since Smitty's fierce steadiness was actually the first thing that differentiated us from any of the other groups. As soon as Smitty came in, we really had a feel. We really started to cook. Plus, we liked him. It was pretty tough in those days, and Smitty knew from tough. Ken also categorically announced that Smitty would wind up causing trouble among us, but that never happened. As it turned out, actually, Smitty stayed with me longer than any of the others. Longer than Ken. And it was the only parting without bitterness, too.

Anyway, by the late sixties and this Chicago gig, we were still all pretty good friends. Which was amazing, because we'd already been on the road for a couple of years and we were already pretty fucked up. I was already feeling freaked all the time. I was singing lead by then and fronting the band and I really just couldn't take it. Though I did, of course. I guess I could take it, 'cause I did.

I remember the first time I noticed that if I waved my arm in the air, thirty thousand eyes would follow it. It's the most unbelievable rush to have a crowd be totally responsive. It's like the audience becomes an extension of your own nervous system or something. Oh my God it used to send me. It was both terrifying and totally thrilling. It was a great game too. I started to love to have this physical relationship with the audience. At one point, around the time I'm talking about, I got into this thing of throwing things into the audience. Balloons, tennis balls, when I could get a roadie to pick some up for me. Sometimes I'd go crazy and start throwing anything that was around on stage, speaker cords, stuff like that. The boys would just watch me and smile, though Nicky one night when he'd popped not one but several Black Beauties actually threw his bass, his favorite bass, out into the crowd. Never got it back, of course, and had to be severely lectured by Ken who pointed out he could have cracked somebody's skull.

I know a lot of this stuff must sound corny now, but you have to understand what we came out of. Which I'll tell you about sometime, though I don't feel like going into that now. On that particular tour, we had these great backup singers, these little girls with great pipes who wore these tiny little skirts, you couldn't understand how they moved. And we used to have these buckets full of these shiny sparkles and every once in a while the girls and I would throw these sparkles around and give the guys doing the lights something interesting to work on. The kids loved it. We were pretty hot, really. I mean, I was never that hot later, on my own. I was just a lot more famous. Standing still, I could create the same effect as I used to get wiping myself out. I'd never admit this, but maybe what's been a lot of my trouble is that I got to be so big that this in itself was sufficient to create excitement, so I didn't have to do so much anymore.

That is, I can create that effect in the audience, but of course it doesn't feel the same to me. But then, of course, what does? Yeah, well. I don't want to think about that.

It's funny, you know, at the height of the Ex-Lovers days, we'd get maybe $15,000 for a show. Tops. And we thought that was amazing. Now if I do a summer festival gig or something I get $500,000. Half a million bucks. I can't fucking believe it, it's so absurd. Yeah, well, I don't want to think about that either.

The night of the Chicago gig was just like any other night and when we got to the hotel I got into the shower—I used to spend like an hour, literally, in the shower after a show, I don't know whether it was to wash it out or to black it out, anyway I was there in the shower completely spaced out and everything and somebody came into the bathroom, one of the backup singers, Georgie, I think, and started yelling "Casey, Casey."

So I turned the water off and stuck my head out and she told me something had happened to Nick who was completely freaked out and did I know what he had taken.

I said, What do you mean, freaked out? and she said he wouldn't come out from under his bed. Which I remember I then repeated stupidly, He won't come out from under his bed? like it was a joke. But then I could tell from her face it was no joke.

So I got out of the shower and just put a towel around me and walked down the hall to Nick's room and everybody was in there, Michael and Will and Smitty and Ken and the three backup singers and even a couple of roadies, it was ridiculous, staring at the bed that Nick was under.

There was a discussion going on as to whether he should be pulled out. Ken was in favor of pulling him out. A couple of people wanted to call a doctor but Ken absolutely vetoed that—he would, that bastard—he was already in a state of perpetual clinical paranoia about the press.

The other two backup singers were on their knees next to the bed, cooing something or other. Michael was sitting on a chair with his head in his hands.

41

When they finally noticed I walked in, Will called out from the other side of the room, "Casey, is it a party night?"

"What are you talking about?" I said.

Some girls, they told me, had been waiting at the stage door and as Michael and Smitty and Nick got into the car, the girls were holding glassine envelopes and calling out "Do you want to spend the night?" Smitty had ignored them but Michael and Nick had taken the envelopes before getting into the car. Once they had driven away Michael had thrown his envelope out the window, but Nick, apparently, had ingested, swallowed, gulped, most likely snorted whatever was in his.

"Of course, we don't know for sure that that's what happened," said Will.

"He was okay during the show," said Smitty.

"He was particularly good during the show," said Michael. "Maybe he'd already popped something or other."

"Won't he talk?" I asked.

"No," several of them said.

"I can't believe it," I said. Everybody knew what I was talking about. We'd decided long ago never to take drugs from any strange kids. Just that week everyone was telling us there was marijuana sprayed with all kinds of shit going around that was making people ill and we'd talked about it. I was the one who was the most vehement about it since I was sick of everybody fucking up on stage. Not that I didn't take drugs on stage myself since at that time nothing could have gotten me out of the dressing room without a Librium and a drink, but I felt a need to draw a line between the functional and the recreational when it got out of hand. I'd talked to Nick particularly. Nick always had to be talked to particularly. Nick was the kid, one of a bunch, of one of those gin-on-the-kitchen-counter semi-Boho suburban mothers, and you'd think that, being brought up so loose and all, he could have rolled with the punches of the life we had better than anyone else in the group, but actually he fell apart almost immediately.

Well, of course that's easy to say now. In fact, to tell you the truth, it makes me sad to realize I think that way now. Getting old, that's for sure. You could say he was falling apart, but the way we thought of it then was that he was just the farthest out. Nick really was outside. And he probably got hit on the most, because he was the cutest. He was the smallest guy in the band, but he had a way about him, something sort of heartbreaking sweet and quiet that on stage was an absolute killer. During the solos, he used to stand there real still playing his bass and then toss his hair back and there'd be, right on cue, this big raunchy thousands-of-girls-screaming sound. It was corny, and we used to make fun of him because of it, but actually we all got a kick out of the action, and maybe a thrill. But so after the show, Nick always had this bevy waiting for him ready and waiting to give him or do him anything, anything at all, and a lot of them would be waiting for him with presents. Once some girl brought him a goddamn fur coat. No kidding.

But anyway, we'd all gotten fucked up so many times from drugs we'd taken from strange people we'd all agreed to cut it out.

"Well, that's not the point now," said Michael.

"Let's be logical," said Ken.

"Acid, mescaline, mushrooms, bad speed, STP, MDA, THC or DMT," said Will.

"It's not DMT," said Smitty, "been going on too long for that shit."

"I think it's acid," said Georgie. "Once I took some at my parents' house and I locked myself in a closet."

"Maybe he had bad acid," somebody said. Then everybody started talking again.

"Wait a minute! Wait a minute!" Michael yelled. "I think he said something."

So we all stayed quiet and Michael lay down on the floor next to the bed and called out "Nick?" but got no answer.

"Hey, Nick, man, won't you answer me?" asked Michael. "Do you want us to leave you alone? Just tell me. If you want we'll just clear out. Just tell me if you're okay?"

But Nick didn't answer. "Can you see him?" Ken asked.

"Ask him if he knows what he took," said Ken.

Michael waved his hand at us for quiet.

"Nicky?" said Michael.

Then Nick said something we couldn't hear.

"What?" said Michael. "A little bit louder," he sang, just like I used to on stage, and we heard Nick giggle.

"That's the idea," said Michael. "It's pretty funny out here, you know. If you came out you might like it. I mean, we're just standing out here like a bunch of assholes."

Then we heard Nick's voice, real muffled. "Is Casey mad?"

"No, darlin', I'm not mad," I called out. "I'm just standing out here with the rest of the assholes."

"Do you want to come out?" Michael asked. "It's just friends out here. Or do you want us to leave? Or do you want everyone but Casey to leave?"

"Can you turn the lights down?" said Nick.

I switched off the overhead.

"Okay, it's cool now," said Michael.

Then Nick said something else, muffled.

"What?" said Michael.

"Don't look at me, okay?" Nick asked in that same strangled voice. "I'll come out, but don't look at me."

"Acid," said Will, sotto voce. A couple of people went shhhh.

"Okay," I called out. "We're not looking, we're just out here talking among ourselves."

So we turned away from the bed and sort of clustered in twos and threes around the room, and sat down on the chairs and on the floors and tried to look normal, which wasn't easy since it was such a little room. It was pretty funny, actually, though we didn't think so at that moment. But it was like some insane charade game or something, our scrambling around to create the right casual tableau especially since half the people there were in their stage duds and I was still in my towel. Michael got up and sat on the bed and Nick crawled out and then sat on the bed too, in the corner. Or huddled, is more like it. Naturally, everybody looked surreptitiously. He was a sight. Definitely on something fierce. All flushed and his eyes incredibly shiny and his hair just standing up on end.

"Can we look now?" Will asked.

"I'd rather you didn't," said Nick in this off-the-planet voice. "I feel kind of weird."

"Do you think you want a doctor?" asked Will.

Ken started to say something but I gave him a raging whispered interdiction and everybody glared at him so he shut up. But no, Nick said, he didn't want to see any doctor. "I'll be okay," he said. "I just feel weird. Just act normal, okay?"

So then the heat was off because it seemed likely Nick would know if he was okay.

He was just like a little kid that night. He was a kid, I guess. We were kids. We all spent most of the night in that little room. Even Ken acted more or less like a human being. Someone asked Nick if he wanted to still go out and hear some blues, but it was too weird for him he said but he would have liked to hear some music. So we sang. It was really pretty hilarious. They'd call up from the desk and ask us to keep it down and we'd say "fine," and hang up and just keep going. I can't even remember what we sang, though we did begin with "Just Walk Away Renee," which was, for some reason no one had ever understood, Nick's favorite song. Smitty played his drumsticks on the night table and I remember Georgie got the backup girls together with some moves and they were really something, really too much. Georgie got incredibly serious about it, just like she did on stage. Georgie used to dance on stage as though she was sewing a hem or something. She'd like, *apply* herself. Anyway, so the girls were doing their moves and Will tried to dance with them, which was so ridiculous that even Nick started laughing and then he was laughing so hard so long even after the song was over we got scared again. "I won't do it again, I won't do it again," Will kept saying, which made Nick laugh even more.

I wonder if Will ever thinks of that night. Probably not. Now that he's a fucking jerkoff Hollywood exec he probably doesn't want to remember anything about those days.

I bet Michael does, though.

Around dawn, everybody went back to their rooms except for Michael and me. We smoked a little marijuana since Nick said he

45

was coming down from whatever he was on and we decided by then it probably had been acid mixed with some bad speed or something, and we were worried about a crash so we thought a little dope would help, which it did. But Nick asked if we would stay a while because he thought he could go to sleep soon. So we kept talking for a while, or singing. Michael I remember did his Chick Berry imitation, which made us laugh. That always used to make us laugh, but that night he found a brilliant flourish and started doing Elmer Fudd doing Chuck Berry. It was incredibly funny. I mean, honest, it makes me laugh now when I think about it.

> *New Jurwzey Turwnpike*
> *In the wee wee hours*
> *I was wollin' swowy*
> *'Cause of dwizzwin' showers . . .*

No, I can't do it. I remember, Nick and I tried to do it that night, but couldn't. Michael was really great at it.

> *So I wet out my wings*
> *And then I bwew my horn.*
> *Bye Bye New Jurwzey*
> *I've become airborne.*
>
> *Now you can't catch me*
> *Baby you can't catch me*
> *'Cause if you get too kwose*
> *You know I'm gone*
> *Wike a cool bweeze.*

God, I hope there's nobody hiding in these fucking sugarcanes listening. I'm through anyway. I'm five minutes over. Not bad. Pretty good. I've earned my day anyway. I've earned my right to be alive, right? I'm doing my job of life today, right?

Nick didn't fall asleep, as it turned out, but we did. I don't even know at what point we stopped talking and dropped off, one on either side of him. I'd gotten under the covers because I was sick of trying to keep that bath towel around my body. Every once in a while I'd wake up and Michael was still sleeping on the other side and Nick lying there in the middle with his eyes wide open and I'd try to wake up too but it was too hard, but several times I put my arm around him and said, just before dropping off, "Are you okay, Nicky?" and he'd say yes, as if he really was.

In the morning, he was fine. When I woke up, Michael was still asleep but Nick was slouched in an armchair, picking his guitar, and he gave me this big sheepish smile. What a smile he had, Nick.

*   *   *

Every day is sunny. Every morning the sky is clear save for thick pure white clouds hovering about the top of the mountains. Most every day there are rainbows.

"I've never seen so many rainbows," says Casey.

"It's the refraction," says Michael.

"In the old tales," says Leslie, "the rainbows hung over places of violent death and were bridges to the other world."

"What other world?" asks Casey.

"You don't want to know," says Michael.

They're in Casey's rented Firebird, driving to a beach on the other side of the island. Michael is in the back. Casey, who is driving, turns her head toward Leslie as if waiting for more. Leslie doesn't continue.

"You guys are funny," says Casey.

"I was thinking maybe Michael is right," says Leslie. "Hearing these myths is like having strange dreams. They stay with you. Maybe they aren't good for you."

"Dreams are supposed to be good for you," says Casey. "I mean, what's the point of art, anyway?"

"To dream your own dream," says Michael. "To send your own dream out into the world."

"Oh, I don't know," says Casey.

"I read in a book," says Leslie, "about a man who had amnesia and had to be taught everything from the beginning. Well, one thing he didn't know was that the dreams he had at night were only his own. He thought everybody went to sleep and had the same dream."

"Just like art," says Michael.

"Hey!" says Casey. "That was my point!"

"Right," says Michael.

"Jesus!" says Casey.

When they get to the beach, they agree to a swim before eating and all three run into the water. Casey tires first, and comes back in to lie on the sand. There isn't much wind that day, so she opens her eyes at the faint sound of Michael drying himself with a towel. He stands looking out to sea where Leslie swims, quite far away, from one large rock to another. Casey leans on her elbows to look too.

"I can't believe how Leslie can be this pregnant and have so much stamina," says Casey.

"Leslie loves the ocean so much I sometimes think it takes more energy from her to be out of it than in it," says Michael.

"I like Leslie," says Casey.

"She likes you a lot," says Michael.

"Why?" asks Casey.

"Are you kidding or are you fishing?" says Michael.

"Self-diagnosis: pathological narcissism," says Casey.

He sits down next to her and surveys her face. "Have you put on sunscreen?" he asks.

"Yeah," she says.

"You look like you need more. It's pretty treacherous on a day like this."

"It's funny you've become so . . ." she hesitated.

"So what?" asks Michael.

"I don't know. Maybe it's from your relationship with Sebastian," says Casey.

"No," says Michael. "You just never checked out that aspect of my personality."

"Or maybe it's because you're going to have your own child," says Casey.

"Do you ever think about that?" says Michael.

"I think about it sometimes," says Casey.

"I think you'd be a very good mother," says Michael.

"You're kidding," says Casey.

"No," he says, "I'm not kidding. But then I've always thought better of you than you did."

"Did you?" she asks, as if she really wants to know.

"Yeah, I always did," he says.

"Mm," she says.

"Are you starting to feel better?" he asks.

"Yes," she says. "I feel much better than I did. Much less nervous, you know."

"You'll see," he says, "after a while here it'll come to seem to you that there's much less to be nervous about than you imagined."

"Is that what happened to you?" she asks.

He doesn't answer.

"I'm sorry," she says. "We don't have to talk about it."

"No," he says. "I was just thinking. I don't know. It really wasn't an act of will on my part."

"You never did want to give yourself any credit for anything."

"Mm, well, maybe that's it," he says. "But I don't think so. It wasn't an act of will because it wasn't a choice."

"Why not?" she says. "Sometimes I think of everything you gave up and I can't even believe you did it. I mean, it's amazing. It's quite impressive."

"I didn't really give up anything," he says, "except wanting to die."

"Did you really want to die?" she asks.

"Yeah," he says. "I think I did. So giving up the drugs and all the rest was just a function of giving up wanting to die."

"Did you really want to die?" she asks again.

"Yeah," he says.

"I'm sorry," she says.

"Why? It wasn't your fault," he says.

"I don't know," she says. "I know you stayed on long past the point when you wanted to quit."

"Stayed on in the band, you mean?"

"Well, yeah," says Casey.

"Oh, I just chose my poison," he says.

50

He lies down on the sand too, and Casey leans back.
"Are you hungry?" he asks.
"Yeah. Pretty," says Casey.
"Leslie's swimming in, we can eat soon," he says.
They both close their eyes.
"I think you should at least put some on your face," he says.

*　　*　　*

I'm starting to feel a little better, I guess. I'm not even sure, but I think when I wake up in the morning the panic is not as bad. It's not that grab you by the throat and squeeze panic. The thing is: Am I better or am I narcotized by Pacific sunshine? Both, maybe. But it's as if everything that hurts me is starting to recede. I don't know. Maybe not. Maybe I'm just getting some sleep and that helps. It doesn't hurt not to be drinking.

Man, I am tough. Aren't I, though? I'm always much tougher than I think I am.

Every morning now I come out here and lie on this chair and stare at that fucking ocean, and that ridiculous blue sky, and it doesn't feel so bad. It doesn't feel so bad to be alone, that's for sure, I never thought I'd like it so much, being alone.

The advantage of leaving New York so fast was that no one has my phone number here. They call at Michael and Leslie's and I get the messages and I just don't call back. I suppose I'd better do something about Anthony, though, or he's liable to just show up here. I really don't want to see him. Especially not here. I feel bound to him by sickness. Though he means me well, I know, in his own way.

Maybe my anger at Anthony has nothing to do with Anthony. In a sense, I'm better off with him than I've been with anyone. I mean, calmer. He's much too civilized to ever prod me into ugly scenes, and of the wrong class, to boot. The angrier he is, the more courteous. No ugly scenes, no tantrums, rages, humiliating confrontations. Why am I bored? Maybe that's what I'm angry about, is that so far he's succeeded in preventing me from destroying him. What fun is that, a love affair in which you don't get to destroy either your lover or yourself or, preferably, in some really thrilling fireworks, both of you? You think I'm kidding? I'm not kidding.

Well, okay, I'm kidding.

Oh, this is stupid, but a sign of health too. I haven't made any jokes to myself in a long time. Actually, I feel better than I have for a long time. I'm just not used to feeling so relaxed. Relaxed, that's what I am. I haven't been able to afford to relax in years. Even now when I think of it, I look for that familiar column of anxiety at the center of my body. It scares me to be without it, as though it were my life center or something. Maybe it has been. Anyway, calming down is so foreign to me that it's really difficult to distinguish between relaxed and tired and listless. Maybe all these things.

If I get totally relaxed, will I crash? And here there'll be no one to take care of me.

Well, I suppose Michael and Leslie would take care of me. But as it is they're being so nice to me that I feel uncomfortable no matter how many assurances I get from either of them that it's okay.

I don't know if it's completely okay. For instance, I don't know for sure what effect it has on Michael to have me around. I know, though, that there is something not completely honest between us. Our pasts, for example, have been so entangled with one another's. And yet we talk very little about anything in the past. Of course, I don't initiate it, but he doesn't either. The thing is, I don't know whether Michael's managed to shape up by leaving all that behind him and he just doesn't think about it anymore or if it's bad for him to think about it. Or if he doesn't talk about it for my sake.

I wonder how pathetic I must seem. Maybe I seem very pathetic.

Sometimes I see something in his eyes that could be either pity or tenderness.

Sometimes I avoid looking in his eyes. He avoids mine, too, I think. I'm talking to him and he averts his glance. But I don't know for sure, because he always did that. In a way, he's less weird than he used to be. He's always had a strange manner. He certainly is much more normal than he used to be. Whatever normal means. To be precise, he acts much more normal.

Well, maybe that's not true.

He's as confusing as he's always been. He looks much better than he did, that's for sure. I mean, in the last couple of years before he left the band. Although there was something I always liked about the way he looked when he was really wasted. It's funny, all of that doesn't show on his face now. That's part of it. And he has that island tan and everything. Tawny, he looks kind of tawny. But there's something sort of open about his face now. In a way I like it better, in a way it embarrasses me. I mean, it makes me feel sorry for him. Which is stupid, of course. But it's definitely as though something died in him. I think he's wrong: he didn't give up wanting to die. Some part of him died to enable him to live. He told me that night in New York that he'd gone to AA. Which I couldn't believe. I just couldn't imagine Michael sitting in an AA meeting in that small Connecticut town. That must have been tough, was all I said, but I guess he knew what I meant because then he said that what made it work was when you stopped thinking about the differences between you and all the other people there and started to think about the similarities.

I guess you have to travel a pretty long road to get to that point.

Sometimes I say I wish I were like other people, lived like other people. But I never mean it. I can't really kid myself that much. I just mean I wish I didn't have this special pain only I have. But I never wish I weren't me. It's as though he's allowed himself to be broken. I don't know how deep that goes, though, or how necessary it may be. I'm real careful, which is maybe one of the reasons why I sometimes don't look at him. I don't know how fragile he is. Maybe I feel myself to be dangerous.

For instance, I notice, he's very seldom ironic with Leslie. There was a time when Michael was never not ironic, not for a second.

In bed, he was just silent. Almost always.

Sometimes I try to think exactly when Michael and I stopped sleeping together, but I can't remember. I mean, after the thing we had was over. We still went to bed a few times. I know there was a point when I decided I wouldn't sleep with anybody in the band at all. For one thing they were all fucking all these groupies and getting all these diseases. God, how I hated that, the whole thing, all these girls hanging around waiting, just waiting. They weren't the prettiest girls, that's for sure. They were just easy. That's what they were there for. I could never believe that Michael, him especially, could be willing to be so upfront about it. Although, certainly, Ex-Lovers was pretty tame by comparison with other bands. I remember, when we'd be in the same hotel with other groups, the girls actually lined up at the guys' doors. And backstage, they were always around, in droves, in those days, wearing tiny little skirts and glittering stockings, see-through blouses, sci-fi makeup, desperate eyes. Once we shared the bill with some Southern band that was hot at the time and I remember having to walk by them on our way to the stage, all these big guys, five of them it must have been, leaning against the corridor wall, with these little groupies all in a row, going down on them.

Yeah, well. Rattle and roll.

Anyway, I decided it was a bad idea to sleep with Michael. Which may seem comical, that it took me that long to figure out it was a bad idea, but I was so fucked up in those days. Though the truth is, I used to also just want a little comfort at night and there was a time when I just couldn't sleep alone. I would have gotten into bed with anybody, and sometimes I did, to just not sleep alone. It wasn't groupies, though. It was guys I'd run into. I don't know. It may not seem like that big a distinction, I guess. In the sixties, there was a difference.

Then I started this long period when I was so weird about sex I didn't want to sleep with anyone I knew. I was in a phase where I was having horrible stage fright. I was relentlessly terrified of the crowd. By then Will had left and I started playing keyboards again, which really didn't add much to our sound, because I really wasn't that good, although of course the kids loved it, but what did they know? No, it was so I could turn away. But even so, my hands would shake. I'd have trouble playing because my hands were shaking so much. I'd rush the beat, I was so scared I couldn't even hear anything. Finally I was screwing up so bad on the tempo that I changed the whole setup on stage so I could see Smitty. In between the shows I'd spend the whole time trying to rearrange my head about this thing. I used to talk to this psychiatrist on the phone every day but that would only freak me out more because I started having these uncontrollably wild ideations about crowds, where I was like trying to have positive fantasies about crowds but each one would always become too frightening to tolerate. Anyway, I became so obsessed with this I could never have sex without thinking of a crowd. I mean, I couldn't come otherwise.

So that's when I stopped sleeping with anyone I really liked. It's not that anybody could read my mind, and I never told anyone, but it was just too weird, and too ruthless. Until Anthony, of course. But Anthony would be into that, actually, if he knew. It's just the sort of thing he would go for. I mean, not that I go through that anymore. But I tune out, that's for sure, and my suspicion is that Anthony knows that, and doesn't just put up with it. That he actually gets off on it. That he wouldn't want it any other way. And I'll tell you something weird: I don't know whether it's a function of his sexuality or of his affection for me. I can think of it as a kind of kinky thing, he's getting off on my mind being elsewhere, or I can think of it as a rather extraordinary acceptance on his part of who and what I am, and I haven't a clue which it is. Although it could be both, of course. Or neither. Maybe I don't even get him at all.

I know I did go to bed with Michael once during that period. A sad occasion, but my just deserts for having gotten between the covers with someone whose veins were filled with smack. It was endlessly unsatisfying. But by then most nights had become sad occasions, for him too, I bet. I don't remember if that was the last time. I wonder if he remembers. He must remember.

Of course I remember the last time I went to bed with Nick, but I don't like to think about that. And, all right, aside from what happened with Nick, I guess it's horrible anyway to think of the sex you had with someone who died.

Okay. Let's change the subject.

Making love with Nick was like wrestling, or going to bed with a panther cub or something. He had all this nervous energy and he always seemed to have more bones and angles and sharp places than any other human being. He could do it for days, too. One time I think I spent about three days in bed with him. In between, he'd play his guitar.

Yeah, well, Nick was outside, all right.

Sometimes I feel as if they all died. They all died except me, one way or another they all died and left me alone.

*　　*　　*

"Hi!" Michael calls out.

Casey, who is lying by the side of the pool, hears him and takes off her earphones.

"Hi. Where's Leslie?"

"At the house. Domestic problems."

"Do you want something to drink? Do you want to go in?"

"No," says Michael. "This is fine." He sits down on a chair and tilts it back. They're facing away from the ocean, toward the mountains.

"Hot today," says Casey. "I've been spending a lot of time in the water."

"You don't like swimming in the ocean?"

"No," says Casey. "I go to the beach a lot, but to swim I come in here. I have a whole routine now."

"You do?" says Michael. "What's your routine?"

"Well," says Casey. "Well, actually, I don't know if I really do have a routine. But I've developed some habits. Like I walk on the beach, and sometimes in the morning I lie out on a deck chair on the beach side of the house."

"Is that what you do first thing?" asks Michael.

"Yeah," says Casey. "Unless I feel really bad. Then I go for a walk or a run right away. Unless I'm feeling *really* bad, in which case I try to go back to sleep."

"Mm," says Michael. "I can never go back to sleep."

"I take a Dalmane," says Casey. "It's great to drink less because now I can take more drugs for on-the-spot relief."

"Oh," says Michael. "And have you been feeling that bad a lot?"

"No," says Casey. "Not in the last week or ten days. I've really started to get better."

"It's because you're getting healthy," says Michael.

"Yeah," says Casey. "I guess I'm getting healthy, come to think of it."

"Your mind follows," says Michael.

"Yeah, maybe," says Casey. "I hope so."

"You look great," says Michael.

"Oh, please, I look terrible," says Casey.

"You look better than I've ever seen you," says Michael.

"Please. Don't make me feel bad," says Casey.

They say nothing for a moment.

"I feel incredibly old," says Casey.

After a pause, Michael says, "Yeah, me too, usually."

"Although it has nothing to do with age," says Casey. "Sometimes I look at Leslie and I think she'll always be young."

"It's true," says Michael. "I've thought of that. Though you know, that's both good and bad."

"I suppose."

"But it's true there's something unharmed about Leslie."

"Unharmed?" says Casey.

"Yeah, undamaged. Like her soul, or if you want to be more prosaic about it, her psyche, is undamaged. But I always think if anybody's got a soul, it's Leslie."

Casey laughs. "The rest of us don't?"

"No. I mean, I never think of myself as having a soul. I mean, something bigger than myself to dip into as an organizing principle. Do you?"

"No," Casey admits. But then she adds, "Except maybe on stage."

"That's true," says Michael. "I hadn't thought of that."

"Well," says Casey. "Maybe that's a lot of bullshit."

"No," says Michael. "It's true."

"It's just the metaphor, soul, it's so grandiose. But something does happen on stage."

"Yeah," says Michael. "It's true, the metaphor's grandiose.

But out here there's no one to slap your fingers so you can be as purple as you want, you know."

"Well, I think this unexpected purple thing suits you," she says.

"Yeah, maybe my speech will get really rich, you know, in another year or two I'll sound like Orson Welles."

"I like it that you talk more," says Casey.

"I try," he says.

"You consciously try, you mean?"

"Yeah," he says. "With people I like."

"It's true," says Casey. "You'd become very silent." He doesn't reply. "Do you want to talk about all that, those years?" she asks.

"I don't know," he says.

"Well, it's up to you," she says. "You don't have to."

"I'd like to be able to, actually," says Michael. "I wish I could reconcile myself with that part of my life you represent."

"What part is that?"

"A lot I guess," he says. "Most of it."

"Do you ever think about playing?" she asks.

"Performing, you mean?" says Michael. "No. I stopped playing, you know."

"Yeah, I know," says Casey.

"Or writing any songs. But do you know what I've been doing lately?"

"What?"

"Playing the violin."

"You're kidding," says Casey.

"No," he says. "Sometimes I wonder if maybe I could start myself going again at some point."

"You like practice really seriously?"

"Yeah, I really do. Every morning."

"You're kidding. You really do?" Casey sits up.

Michael glances at her, then looks back at the mountains. "I hadn't played in so long, I'm really unbelievably terrible," he says. "But I've been doing scales and so forth every morning for the last few months."

60

"Gee," says Casey. She lies down again. "I think that's fantastic. I'm almost tempted to offer to play with you."

"I'm not up to playing with you yet," says Michael.

"You'd be surprised," she says. "It's been a really long time since I played myself. And I haven't played any classical for years, not for years."

"Do you miss it?" he asks.

"No, I'm relieved," she says.

"Really?" he says. "I keep thinking that if I could just get myself back to the point where I can get through a Beethoven sonata I'd be all set."

"Oh," she says, "no. I didn't mean about music, or certainly not about Beethoven. I was talking about work, which I guess lately seems to have so little to do with music. I mean, I'm relieved not to work. I've just been working for so long and trying to write songs and trying to keep my voice in shape and taking care of the business of it and everything and it's just been a horrible grind for so long that now I have this, like, unbelievable negative tropism about all of it."

"Well," he says, "it goes away. It'll go away when you feel better."

"I don't know," says Casey. "Well, it's true, at least now I can at least listen to music. Though I only listen to classical. It's funny, I never thought of playing. I think it's amazing you're doing that. I think it's great."

"Yeah, well," says Michael. "I justify my existence a little."

Casey laughs. "You don't think your existence is justified otherwise?"

"You tend to fall into a pretty hedonistic thing out here," says Michael.

"Yeah, I can see that," she says.

"Don't want to have too much pleasure," says Michael. "Don't want to get carried away, or anything."

"Yeah, right," says Casey.

"I think I'll have some juice or something," says Michael.

"Okay. Me too."

"What would you like?"

"Oh, anything," she says. "I'm thirsty, but I can't move."

Michael comes back with two glasses.

"Papaya and guava," he says.

Casey sits up. "Jesus. I can't believe how much of this shit I drink now."

"Do you want to do something?"

"Like what?" she says.

"A drive or a walk?"

"Okay," she says.

"Which?"

"Uh, I don't know. Maybe we should go for a little walk on the beach and while we're walking we'll decide."

"Okay," he says. "Or are you hungry?" he asks. "Leslie's expecting to make us some lunch. Are you hungry yet?"

"No, not just yet," she says. "Are you?"

"No," he says. "Not yet." He takes off his T-shirt and his rubber sandals. They finish their juice and head toward the beach.

"It's really calm today," she says as they approach the ocean.

"So," he says, "Casey, what do you do next in the morning?"

"When?" she says.

"After you've gone on a walk or a run."

"Oh," she says. "I come back and sometimes I eat something.

"Then what?" he asks.

"Then I take a shower."

"Then what?"

*　　*　　*

been doing this all my adult life and it's destroying me but I don't know how to do anything else.

And how long am I going to get away with it, anyway? How long am I going to get away with looking and singing like a kid? But I don't know what else there is for me to do. I can't even think of anything.

Maybe that's why all these people are here eating curd and so forth is because they can't think of anything either.

I think that's why Michael and Will and Smitty really left the group anyway, whatever reasons they may have thought they had. It's because they knew they were getting too old. They couldn't picture themselves in any possible future if they stayed on.

I've always felt so guilty about the whole thing. I mean, my winding up fronting the band, and then eventually it was just me and the band was a backup band. It was never planned, it happened little by little. It could have gone any other way. Or not. Who knows? I don't.

Jesus, I'm getting the willies just thinking about all this. It's having to make these fucking phone calls. I feel I just can't face anything.

The thing is, could my whole life have gone some other way? Is there some other turn I should have taken?

Occasionally, I think of that day on the Vineyard with Michael and Nick and it seems to me that just one word or one gesture or even one glance could have made everything different. I mean, I know it could have.

Oh, man, fuck this. I'm not going to get into this.

> *And when it comes to thinkin' about*
> *Anything but my baby,*
> *I just don't have time,*
> *Ain't got time for nothin' else.*

Okay. Let's consider our options. Should I make some phone calls or should I go to bed?

* * *

Michael and Leslie's house is an analogue of Casey's, spacious, sparsely furnished with low, light furniture in whites and beiges, but here and there are touches of Sebastian's preoccupations: picture books and toy trucks. On a kitchen counter, seashells neatly encircle a little toy piano.

"What else can I do?" Casey asks.

She and Leslie are clearing up in the kitchen. Michael is in Sebastian's room, reading a bedtime story.

"I think that's it," says Leslie. "I think you should sit down and drink your tea."

"I don't mind. I sort of like it, actually," says Casey. "I never get a chance to do stuff like this."

"Clean the kitchen, you mean?" says Leslie. "It's true, I sort of like it in a way. I mean, for someone like me who does nothing else it's a source of accomplishment."

"It's not true that you do nothing else."

"Well, these days," says Leslie, patting her belly. "But, you know, I've never done much. I've always been sort of a waste. Just wanted to have fun."

"Christ!" says Casey. "You think having fun is a waste?"

"Well, you know, I wish I could create something sometimes."

"Everybody who creates something wishes they could be having fun."

"Don't some of them have fun?" says Leslie.

"I don't know," says Casey. "If so, I never run into them."

Leslie bends down to put powder in the dishwasher.

"Are you uncomfortable?" Casey asks.

"No," says Leslie. "I like it. I really like being pregnant."

"I think it's incredible what you've done for Michael," says Casey. "That's a lot right there, saving a life."

"No, I didn't, you know," says Leslie. But she looks pleased, and smiles at Casey. "I was just there."

"You're funny, Leslie," says Casey. "You never want to take credit for anything."

"No, that's not true," says Leslie. "For example, I do think I'm a good mother. It's the one thing I can do. In my own way, I mean." Leslie looks around the kitchen and says, "That's it," and they both sit down at the table where mugs of tea are steaming.

"This is such a luxury for me," says Casey. "Just to be quiet like this."

She puts both her hands around her mug.

"Are you okay?" Leslie asks.

"Why? Do I look sad?"

"You did for a moment. Sometimes you do, for a moment."

"Yeah, well," says Casey. "Devils. Lots of devils around, waiting."

"Do you ever want to have a child?" Leslie asks.

"I don't know," says Casey.

"They keep away the devils," says Leslie.

"I don't know," says Casey. "I guess I've never been in a situation where I could have, so I've never really thought it through. Actually, these last few weeks are the most peaceful I've had in a long time. Ever, maybe."

"It's great having you around," says Leslie. "I hope you stick around."

"That's nice," says Casey. "You're really nice. I know I must be an interruption here. I mean, I've caused you so much trouble."

"Oh no," says Leslie. "I really like it that you're here. And it's really nice for Michael to have a pal besides me. He likes my friends but he never really becomes pals with any of them. It's hard for him."

"Yeah," says Casey. "I think we all got used to not having any pals." She takes a sip of her tea. "I guess," she says, "having a baby is sort of guaranteeing a perpetual pal."

67

"Well," says Leslie. "I don't know. They're so much work. But it's perpetual love."

"Why do you say that?"

"I don't know."

" 'Perpetual love' would make a good song," says Casey.

"What's a good song?" asks Michael, coming back into the kitchen.

"Never mind," says Casey.

Michael pours himself some tea.

"No, what?" he asks.

"No, you always thought my song ideas were crummy."

"That's not true," he says.

"Girls' songs, you all used to say with incredible contempt."

"Well," says Michael. "I've mended my ways and come to think that girls' songs are not so bad."

"I wonder," says Casey.

"No, really," says Michael.

Something about his expression makes both women laugh.

"Sappy, is the word you guys used to put me down with."

"Oh, God, that's right," says Michael.

"That's terrible," says Leslie.

"Yeah!" says Casey.

"It's true, we were pricks," says Michael. "We teased too hard."

"I don't think you were teasing."

"No, it was teasing," says Michael.

"I don't know," says Casey.

"But it's because we were jealous," says Michael.

Casey smiles and shakes her head but says nothing.

"It's true," says Michael.

"Plus maybe they were all in love with you, Casey," says Leslie. "They were like little boys."

"Bull's-eye," says Michael.

"Oh, come on," says Casey. "I know my songs weren't as good as yours or Will's."

"Well . . ." says Michael.

Casey laughs.

"No," says Michael. "I'm kidding."

"Oh, it's all right," says Casey.

"Michael, that's terrible," says Leslie.

"No, it's okay," says Casey.

"You know I'm kidding, right?" asks Michael seriously.

"Sure," says Casey.

"No, really," Michael insists because he can see she doesn't believe him. He clasps his head. "God, why did I do that?"

"No, I believe you," says Casey very solemnly.

"You're arranging your features to look convincing," declares Michael.

"Well, I've got to be good at something!" says Casey. She turns to Leslie and puts on the same earnest expression. "Don't you think I'm good at this?" she says.

Michael and Leslie laugh. "That's far out," says Leslie. "I want to try it." She turns to Michael. "There's something I've been meaning to tell you," she starts, but she can't keep a straight face. "I can't," she says, laughing.

"No, you have to really believe it," says Casey. "That's the trick, you have to talk yourself into it for a second. Watch."

*   *   *

It was when we went on tour that everything started going wrong. We weren't equipped, is what it was. Not that anybody's equipped, really, but we were just a bunch of college kids and to boot we had this compulsion to stay cool throughout the whole thing, to maintain our ironic stance, and that really cost us a lot, in a way. I mean, in other bands, there were always a lot of explosions and people yelling at one another and then they'd all go and get really grotesquely drunk together and that would be it. But we were too cool for that in the Ex-Lovers. That's what we called ourselves—Michael and Nick had come up with that name and it plagued us for our entire career to have chosen such a dorky name.

Anyway, almost right away there began to be trouble among us, but everybody was just too fucking cool to ever really talk about anything so everything would just fester. Well, not right away. At first, when we were just playing clubs, we had a great time. But then we had this minor hit and went on tour and that was really the end of us. There's so little to do in between shows. So much waiting around in airports. Everybody's tired all the time. So there are all these intrigues and shifting alliances and paranoia abounds. Everyone was constantly mad at everyone else. I was mad at them all almost all the time. Maybe it was because I felt guilty; as soon as the group became Casey and the Ex-Lovers it stopped being fun for me. I'm not kidding. Or so I told various shrinks later. Well, but maybe I'm kidding myself. And all this is camouflage to obscure the incredible narcissistic spin I then went into.

I don't know. We were so exhausted, for one thing. That was a lot of it. Especially on the first tour, we had no money, and Ken had planned the most penny-pinching tour in the history of rock 'n' roll. We'd play a town and then go back to the rattiest hotel where we'd have to share rooms, sometimes two, sometimes three to a room, and the next morning be back on a plane. You never had a minute alone, you never had a day's break, you always felt so weary that you could never get yourself to have a real meal. And every day you'd wake up in another awful place. After a couple of weeks we didn't know where we were anymore. Everyone was taking a lot of drugs and drinking, and the boys used to have an unbelievable amount of sex. This made me furious. I thought it was incredibly uncool. I felt, I don't know, unbelievably demeaned. Which, when I think of it now, is sort of bizarre. Maybe it was because I'd slept with them myself. Not Will, I'm glad to say I never went to bed with Will. Something about him always turned me off. Too calculating, I guess. You've got a lot going for you if you have the kind of bulldozer ambition Will's always had, but not sex appeal. I mean, unless you win really big, of course. If you have enough power, even pathological ambition can seem attractive or even endearing. But Will didn't have enough talent to win that big. Ambition's not enough, after all. Even in rock 'n' roll. Anyway, I don't know. Maybe I'm wrong. Maybe it's only with hindsight that it makes sense that Will gave me the creeps. All I knew at the time is that he turned me off physically and, mainly, that he seemed like a drag.

In any event, I didn't have that same neurotic possessiveness about him that I felt about Michael and Nick, which was all the more poisonous because I hid it very carefully. I mean, I knew I was being totally uncool. Of course, you might suggest the plain fact is that I was jealous, but I don't know. It may have been less jealousy with regard to them than to their freedom. I mean, maybe I would have liked to have done the same thing. Though I could see, almost right away, that it drove them crazy. I mean, quite literally crazy, especially Nick.

Nick, I guess, was really the least equipped for it all. He was always the strangest of any of us anyway. Even when I first met him in school he was already truly strange. He just hardly spoke, for one thing. Literally, he hardly talked and hardly ever laughed, and when he did there was something sort of painful about it. Although at that point, in the mid-sixties, it didn't seem all that remarkable since a lot of people had truly strange demeanors and it was always hard to say who was eccentric and who was truly mad and who had regular temporary teen angst and who was in a serious state of anguish.

I don't know. Of course, it could be that I've exaggerated this aspect of Nick's personality over the years. The other thing is, although it didn't seem at all strange at the time, he smoked an unbelievable amount of marijuana. Unbelievable. Everybody knew that Nick had to have the bed closest to the window at the hotel. And he'd pull it right next to the window and leave the curtain open. Everybody used to kid him about it and he wouldn't really explain all this, but maybe it's because he grew up in the suburbs and just felt too trapped in all these cities. Anyway, he'd wake up in the morning and light up a joint first thing and lie in his bed looking out the window. If he woke up too late to have his joint in bed he'd smoke it in the car on the way to the airport. If need be, he'd smoke it on the plane in the bathroom which made everyone else go crazy with paranoia since this was still the sixties and everybody lived in perpetual fear of being busted, especially us, traveling around looking wasted with all these guys who had really long hair, and we figured they were just waiting to get us, which they were, of course. It's the only time I've seen Nick have an argument with anyone, which he did, if you can call it that, with Ken, who was trying to get him to cut it out and Nick just kept saying "No, man, I won't." Which was typical of Nick since of course he could have just lied about it or told Ken to fuck off or something.

I think what finally happened is that Michael told Ken to fuck off, because it was horrible to see Ken badgering Nick like that. It was so obvious that Nick didn't have a clue how to defend himself from someone like Ken, or from the rest of the world, for that matter, which I guess is why he was so weird in the first place.

Anyway, I can't explain why we didn't find Nick's behavior more peculiar, except that we were young and that's how it was then. We each had the right to be as freaky as we wanted to be. For all we knew, Nick's behavior was part of his thing, his youthful affectation. Mainly, it was interesting to observe. He was almost, it's hard to explain, autistic. I guess we just ascribed it to his being so stoned all the time and it just didn't occur to us that the reason he stayed stoned was that he was so fucked up.

Or maybe he wasn't that fucked up. What do I know? As I say, by current standards he was incredibly fucked up, but those were other times. Or whatever.

But, anyway, Nick and those girls was something fierce. When I say he woke up and smoked a joint I should say there was always a girl in his bed, sometimes several. Though at various times I was told by people who shared rooms with him that often he didn't even fuck the girls. Nick always turned the girls on too so there was always a weird scene when we left with some girl standing there stoned like a zombie and we used to make jokes about what their parents would say when they got home that morning. Nick never laughed at the jokes. Sometimes he'd just walk away. He must have been ferociously lonely, I realize now, and to tell you the truth I can't think about that too much because it makes me want to cry and I don't want to cry over all this old shit, I just couldn't stand it. Too many horrible things happened to cry over.

Besides, I guess we were all gruesome lonely.

I know I was drinking in the morning. Though I wouldn't have called it that. I had hot toddies, if you can believe it. I'd go down to the hotel bar first thing in the morning and ask for a hot toddy, which of course they never had, so then I'd ask for a tea with rum and I got used to having problems so I'd carry my own stupid tea bags. Naturally, I had my own bottle. A bottle of rum for the morning and a bottle of tequila for the evening. Before going on stage, those days, I found Librium and tequila to be the right cocktail. Jesus, I must have had insides made of steel. But, anyway, in the A.M., I didn't feel so hot. And we used to get up so early, God, in the winter it would still be dark. Every morning there'd be a big hassle just to get these people to boil some water because they'd always say the kitchen was closed, but most mornings I won and I'd sit there like a smoldering zombie drinking this tea and rum and trying to get myself together.

Everybody knew that was where to find me. After a while, everybody would just gather there instead of in the lobby which finally began to really be an unbearable drag since other people would drink and then be drunk in the car on the way to the airport, which was too much for me. Believe me, I was not in a mood to party. I needed to have, like, complete silence in the morning. So when they'd come down and sit next to me at the table I wouldn't talk to any of them.

It seems incredible now, I guess. I mean, there was some sort of hypertolerance of everybody's peculiarities, so after a while everyone knew there was to be no talking at that table in the morning so we'd all sit there in silence, looking like hell, we were *in* hell—have you ever seen a sleazy hotel bar first thing in the morning?—most of the time the chairs were still on the tables. We'd sit there in hell in stony silence and drink.

It wasn't just Nick. We were all crazy. I'm just thinking how several hours later we'd be on stage singing and leaping around and everything. Which in a way was just a different kind of hell, the fire-and-brimstone-drive-yourself-to-perdition hell. That was a lovely hell, the hell you yearned to burn in. It must have made us all crazy really fast, living in these various hells.

At the same time, don't think I don't miss it. Don't think I don't sit here in this ridiculous grown-up beach house on fucking Kaulani and miss those days.

Well, at least I don't drink in the morning anymore. Yeah. Big deal. Great.

*   *   *

"You seem much better," Michael says to Casey.

"Well, yes," says Casey. "I'm up and down, but I think my downs aren't as low."

On the porch Michael is lying on a lounge chair, Casey is sitting on a cushion hugging her knees, and the sun is setting.

"You seem much more relaxed," says Michael, "since you decided to stay."

"I wish," says Casey, "I could figure out what to do about this record."

"When were you supposed to go into the studio?"

"In a couple of weeks," says Casey. "I'm really fucking up because they're getting everything together in New York, locking out a studio and booking musicians, and they're going to be really furious."

"Do you have the songs?" says Michael.

"Well," says Casey. "Yes. Such as they are."

Michael turns to Casey. "You know, I really was kidding the other day."

"I know," says Casey. "Though I don't fool myself, you know, about what I can do. I can't write anything on the level of what you and Will used to do."

"That's not true," says Michael. "Your stuff has something else going for it."

"Well, yeah," says Casey. "Maybe."

"And also, the times have changed. It's harder to write good songs."

"Do you think I should quit?" Casey asks suddenly.

"I don't know," says Michael. He doesn't seem surprised by her question. He's looking, through the screen, at the blood-red sky. "Do you?"

"I don't know," says Casey. "I don't know how long I can go on. I don't know why I should go on."

"Well," says Michael. "That's another question."

"It sort of cheers me up," says Casey, "to see you've answered it."

"What do you mean?" says Michael.

"I mean that it seems clear to you why you should go on."

"No," says Michael. "I just decided one day that being healthy meant not asking myself anymore."

"Oh, God," says Casey. "Then I don't know if I can ever be healthy."

"Well, healthy for me, I mean," says Michael. "Plus, that's the advantage of having a kid around, is that each day seems worthwhile for its own sake, you know. I mean, stuff happens, and you just keep up with it."

"Are you ever bored?" Casey asks.

"Yes," says Michael.

"And then what do you do?"

"Anything," he says. "I wait for it to be over."

"I just figure if I stopped I would have nothing to do. I have no other life. What would I do?"

"Well," says Michael. "It's true, that's a problem I haven't solved. It's the big problem of staying here, you're doing stuff all the time but you're not doing anything. Of course, that sort of thing seems more blatant here, but it's true everywhere in a way."

"God," says Casey. "You've become so Eastern."

"Well, maybe," says Michael. "What the hell? I don't have anything better to do with my mind."

"On the other hand," says Casey, "maybe that's what peaceful is. It's just so foreign to me I automatically assign it to another culture."

"I'm not so peaceful," says Michael.

"You're not?" she asks. "You seem it. You're not?"

76

"No," he says. "I mean, I am in patches. At the beach, for instance."

Casey sighs. "I'm not sure of the difference between relaxed and peaceful."

"No, me neither," he says.

"Really?" she asks.

She waits for him to go on but he doesn't.

"This is just what you used to do," says Casey.

"What?" he says.

"Start saying something interesting and then not continue."

"It's because I have nothing else interesting to say."

"Oh, come on," says Casey. "Get off it."

Michael laughs. "You know," he says, "I'm glad you're here."

"I'd forgotten how much I like you," Casey says.

"Me too," says Michael.

"Actually, I'm lying," says Casey. "I hadn't forgotten. I mean, I'd forgotten, but then I remembered."

"Me too," says Michael.

Casey stands. "I think I'll have a glass of wine," she says.

"Me too," he says.

"Really?" says Casey. "Is that really a good idea?"

"Yes, it's a good idea," he says.

"I don't want to debauch you or anything," Casey calls out on her way to the kitchen.

"So," she says when she returns. "What do you think?"

"About what?" he says.

"About my staying here or going back."

"I thought you'd already decided," he says.

"Well, I just want to know what you think."

He's silent. "I don't know," he finally says. "I don't know if my opinion is worth much."

"I hate it when you say things like that," says Casey. "I detest it."

"Well, but for one thing it's true I really do like having you around, so maybe that colors my view. For another, I made some choices for myself, but I don't know if they're right for you."

"I hate this," says Casey. "When I can't decide anything."

"I thought," says Michael, "that you didn't seem to be in such good shape in New York or when you first got here."

"I was a wreck, you mean. I am a wreck."

"Well," he says. "You're a wreck if you think you're a wreck."

"Do I think I'm a wreck?" Casey asks.

Michael laughs. "Do you?" he says.

"I don't know. I'm getting a little drunk on just a few sips of wine, it's ridiculous."

"Me too," says Michael.

"Really?" says Casey. "You are, really? That's funny."

After a pause Michael says, "I love this time of day."

In the screened-in porch, it's gotten dark, but a few feet away the sand is luminous. Only a sliver of dark-red sun shows at the other end of the ocean.

"It's a little scary," says Casey, waving at the sky.

"It's tremendously violent," he says.

"Though it's so still," says Casey.

"That's what's scary," he says.

"Well," says Casey. "I guess that's why you like it."

"I think you should stay," says Michael.

"What?" says Casey.

"I was thinking of whether I'd evaded your question earlier. It's just hard, you know, to take responsibility, but it just seems to me from everything you've told me that you really could use a break."

"I guess I think I should too," says Casey.

"Well, then, you have your answer," he says.

"I don't know, you know," says Casey, "how much I can get into all this physical fitness stuff. I mean, I'm glad I've been getting the drinking under control. It was worth it just for that, but all this other sort of fanatical health obsession, it really isn't my thing."

"Do you like it here?" Michael asks, not looking at her.

She looks at him. "On this island, you mean?" she says. She looks away. "I don't know if I'd like it here without you. Without you and Leslie. It's too much of a parody of itself, I guess.

Except on vacation, maybe, but to hang around this long, I think it would seem too confining, it would start to drive me crazy. Not enough to do. And, well, also, there's a trail's end thing that I think I'd find depressing, for myself."

"But you're not getting the point about what goes on here," says Michael. "It just seems like a stage set to you and you observe people here like characters in a play, because they aren't like you. But there's something about being on an island like this that goes beyond the cartoon. It goes beyond the physical fitness and health craze. If you don't get that, you're missing the boat on what island lifestyle is all about. It's not a fad, it's an old thing, that has to do with tranquillity and harmonious surroundings and simplicity. Even the New Age mysticism stuff is just plugging into that old need. It's really about healing yourself, if you let it work on you."

"Gee, I never thought I'd hear you sound so earnest about anything," says Casey.

"It's a turnoff?" asks Michael.

"No, you can't ever, ever be a turnoff," says Casey.

"You're thinking about why I'm saying what I'm saying instead of what I'm saying," says Michael.

"How well you know me," says Casey, smiling.

"All right," he says. "I give up."

"Maybe I don't want to heal myself," says Casey.

"Well, I do," says Michael.

"Are you annoyed at me?" asks Casey.

"No," he says. "I'm annoyed at myself because I wish I were more eloquent. But then I've never been able to talk you into anything."

"Well, neither has anyone else," says Casey.

"Just give it a chance," says Michael. "Give yourself a chance."

"I sort of worry that it must be a drag for you and Leslie to have me around so much."

"No, you're never a drag, Casey," he says.

"I mean, I worry that you're both too nice or too polite or you feel sorry for me or something. . . ."

"No, I don't feel sorry for you. And Leslie admires you very much."

"Oh, God, don't tell me that. It's too ridiculous."

"No," he says, "it's not so ridiculous."

"I envy Leslie," she says.

"Do you?"

"Well, yes and no. I mean, in a way I do, but I know I could never be like her."

"Actually," he says. "That's exactly how I feel."

"Really?" says Casey.

The sun disappears.

"Do you think we should have another glass of wine?" Casey asks.

"Half a glass," says Michael.

*   *   *

Am I thinking too much about Michael?

Run a little harder. Run a little faster. My God it's hot today. I'm doing much better, though, at this running. It's true something happens after a little while that's sort of like sex or music. Something takes over. Now it happens almost every day and I've come to depend on it. Well, of course, any new addiction is always welcome.

I don't know how much I run—two, three miles? Maybe more. I try not to think, because there are days on which almost anything I think about is painful, and what's the point of that? The hell with that. Plus there's something about this running that can do something interesting to your mind, if you let it. I don't want to be distracted from the weird altered state I can get into. I guess I've come to get hooked on that as well. Goodness knows I'm always thankful for any alteration whatsoever. Goodness knows it's not easy to come by altered states without drugs. I wonder what I would have said if someone had told me, around 1968 or 1969 or so, that all the kids I knew who used to think that the reason to get up in the morning was principally to blast off on whatever drug they could get their hands on would one day be paying seventy-five bucks an hour to specialists in stress management. I wonder what I would have said if someone had told me in around 1970 that I'd have to live through my twenties and thirties without psychedelics? "You must be kidding! What's the point?" I would have said. And I would have been right.

Maybe it's a bad thing to get hooked on this. I'm so used to worrying about getting hooked on anything that gives me

81

pleasure that I can't always differentiate the good from the bad. Health is such an abstraction, isn't it?

Well, but running does sort of make the rest of it easier. I'm better the rest of the day, that's for sure.

Just wish it weren't so hot.

There have been rapes in these sugarcane fields, sometimes I think about that, because it's so quiet. There's only the sound, now and then, of a plane overhead. When I get near the road there's some traffic, but I like to be inside where it's so still and where it's just the thump of my own feet, which I like. It's funny, I never thought I would like so much to be alone.

Well, at least I'm keeping busy. Michael's theories about islands and spiritual simplicity and all really make me laugh. I think there are a lot of people here working on their bodies because it gives them a structure and then they make up this other stuff to make it seem like a key to something more significant.

But, the key to what, anyway, I want to know, aside from just getting from one day to the next. Though that's a lot, I guess.

Or maybe I just don't know. I've become so fucking self-involved I truly can't imagine anymore how anyone can feel or think differently than I do. I feel like the whole world is just populated with different versions of me.

Well, let the shrinks and the magazine writers work on that. Fact is, somewhere I know that's true. I mean, you couldn't perform otherwise, if you didn't have a sense of your connection with everyone else, whether you're imagining it or not. It would just be meaningless gestures and sounds.

What would I have done if I hadn't done this? I don't even know. Sometimes I think what a jerk I was for choosing something to do that can only suit a seventeen-year-old girl. It's got to degrade from there. Plus, there was a time when it meant something. Even politically, actually, though we never thought of it that way, but there was a possibility for action at least. Going on a stage and wiping yourself out was a form of action. Now it's come to be show business. It gets harder and harder for it to be genuine or authentic in any way.

Maybe it has nothing to do with my age, maybe I've just done it too much. Maybe you use it up.

It certainly seems to me that there's nothing less entertaining than show business.

I get this dull ache in my brain thinking about this stuff.

I remember the very first time I sang with a band, with a real drummer and electric guitars, not folk songs but rock 'n' roll. Jesus, more than twenty years ago. More years than my age then. It was like being shot out of a cannon. You just felt *propelled*. That's what it was like in those years. Especially when the audiences became responsive. No matter how I felt before going on stage soon after the show started I was like floating. The more I surrendered to it, the more I floated. Electric. Like there were millions of volts going through my body. Like my brain was hurtling out into space in a thousand pieces. Better than any drug I've ever had. Better than anything. That's the problem, I guess. Before and after was so bad, so gray, so empty.

Like now.

Well, that's not true.

I think I better watch out about Michael. It's funny, I haven't been vigilant, just because it's been so long since I had any feelings like that about anyone at all. Years. It's amazing to be old enough so that you can say that: years. Also I guess I figured once something has happened with someone and died it stays dead. You can't make another fire out of ashes. Except, sometimes, in your memory or your fantasies.

I guess in a way what happened between Michael and me was in another life. I don't know. I couldn't go for him again, in that way. It's like last decade's clothes—you can see what you liked about them but they're just too hopelessly out of style to wear again. We've evolved too differently in relation to the times. I think he's stuck in some old thing. I mean, I haven't done so well accepting the present but I think Michael's route is a hopeless copout. Even his integrity, in a way, seems anachronistic now. I don't know. I feel sorry for him, that's for sure. But I guess he feels sorry for me, too.

I know the exact night I got hooked for good on rock 'n' roll.

It was the first time we played for a real crowd. Before that, we'd been playing little clubs and coffeehouses. Mainly, we rehearsed. There were a lot of pickup bands around those days, but none of them rehearsed as much as we did. And not just fooling around: we were really disciplined. For the first year or so of Ex-Lovers, what I thought rock 'n' roll was was all of us in a barn playing "You Can't Judge a Book by Its Cover" for hours at a time. I had no idea. No idea. I guess we'd concentrated a lot on the music and the sound. That night was Halloween, and there was a dance at school, soon after we'd formed the band. This is 1966 I'm talking about. I don't know if you know what I mean. It was the most stoned people I'd ever seen to date. Everyone was stoned, the band, the kids, the music, the lighting, the clothes. Those clothes! I can't even believe it when I think about it now. Those feathers and fringes and sparkles and tassels, and skirts so short the girls looked naked. And like this buzz, this hum of fun, before the music got started. And we were . . . I can't even tell you what a great mood we were in. The band was on this powerful combination of controlled substances, I'll tell you that. We started right in with "Spoonful" and it was . . . it was ridiculous. That was Michael and Nick, and all those years they spent drowning in Chicago blues. I mean, it was the two of them who came up with that kind of scorching blues sound with a big syncopated back beat. Later it seemed like nothing special because so many other people were doing it, but at the time, it was something. There was already a lot of blues type bands around, but they sounded kind of wooden compared to us. No kidding. We already knew that. And there was all kinds of weird stuff around. There was still a lot of plain folk sound around, especially on the East Coast, trip music, blue grass, jug band, I don't know what else. Mostly it was folk rock. Meanwhile the ultimate height of soul music was sweeping the country. And we used all that, but we went for it.

And that beat. What it felt like to hear that beat when you were seventeen years old and ready for anything. I mean, the Lawrence Welk show was a happening event at the time, you know? Seems like a joke now, but that was the context. That's what people were listening to on purpose.

Well, let me tell you, that kick drum resonating in your thorax, that was really something. And Michael's Stratocaster wailing like right down the center of your cerebellum. Michael went right into the alternate reality, right during "Spoonful." The speakers were blitzed, of course. We were playing with equipment we'd sabotaged to get all kinds of big, illegal sounds. Michael and I were totally locked with the rhythm section. Nick's bass was locked into Smitty's kick drum like if they were lovers. And Will, I don't know what the fuck he was on, but I've never heard him play piano before or since like he did that night. He didn't have hands, he had hammers. We were in the amen corner, all right. I can't tell you what it's like to sing in front of that kind of rhythm section. I mean, like it was like the wildest, funkiest, most pulverizing thing that had ever happened to me. And by far the sexiest. Shit, it made real sex seem like nothing. Though I didn't think of that at the time. I don't know what I was thinking. My brain wasn't thinking, it was, you might say, kind of sizzling along the ridges of the groove. You know, sort of like a toboggan. I'd never heard Michael sound like that. I'd had no idea that he was capable of having this thing happen to him in front of an audience. He went into this ten-minute solo that was maybe the most savage thing I'd ever heard. We kept it afterward, every time we played that tune he played a ridiculously long solo. In fact, that night had a lot to do with how we configured ourselves as a band. But the main thing was, we were all incredibly turned on. In fact, we were ripped. It wasn't just the drugs. It was the idea of the drugs. And the idea that the audience was just as stoned as we were, if not more. And hearing the music that loud, in that big space. And watching people dance, totally in tune with us. And for the first time I entered that circle, that circle between you and the audience and the music and the drugs and the noise and the heat, in which everything seemed perfectly connected. Perfectly, perfectly connected.

And the other thing that happened that night is that I totally understood the power of that, of being able to produce that. I remember there were some kids who came and stood right in front of the bandstand, and they just, you know, *stood* there. It's easy now to sneer at all that stuff. But I remember those kids standing there that night, all night, as if transfixed. Do you know what it feels like to *transfix* someone? Do you?

*   *   *

The beach is misty and luminous. The sun is low.

Leslie suddenly crouches. "Look," she says to Casey.

"A crab?" says Casey.

Leslie laughs at Casey's tone. "I can tell you're not into the sealife spectacle kind of thing."

"I don't know," says Casey. She too crouches but now it's too late. She stares at the little hole in the sand. "I'm too distracted, I guess."

Leslie smiles at Casey. Casey smiles back and then runs her finger along Leslie's cheek. They both sit back on their haunches.

"It took Michael a while," says Leslie.

"Did it?"

"Yes."

"And what about you?"

"What do you mean?" says Leslie.

"Haven't you always been . . ." starts Casey. "Uh . . ."

"It's California," says Leslie. "I've always lived in a sunny place."

Casey says nothing for a moment. "That's a weird thing to say," she tells Leslie, "about yourself. It's like something someone else says about you."

"You mean you think I'm defining myself in a glib way?" asks Leslie.

Casey laughs. "Yeah, well, maybe," she says.

"I've shut down the systems I don't need," says Leslie. "I don't want to suffer."

Casey stares at Leslie. "You sure are a surprising girl," she says.

Leslie hoists herself back on her heels. "Do you want to keep walking?" she asks.

Casey stands and brushes the sand off her legs. "You don't like to talk about yourself?" she asks Leslie.

"I guess not," says Leslie.

"Amazing," says Casey. "Absolutely amazing."

"There's not so much to talk about," says Leslie.

"Oh sure," says Casey. "Right."

Leslie laughs. "Do you think I'm being coy?"

"No," says Casey. "I mean, I don't know. Just lucky, I guess. I'd give a million dollars to stop thinking about myself for a minute."

"Well, there are ways."

"Oh, Jesus," says Casey, "I hope you're not going to talk to me about yoga or anything."

"No," says Leslie. "I'm not."

They amble down the beach again.

"Music," says Casey. "Music can be a form of pure concentration."

"I guess that's how I feel watching a crab," says Leslie.

"Really?" says Casey.

They walk until night starts falling and the tide rises. The wind rustles in the palm fronds. A weak half-moon materializes, not far from some reddish clouds. Casey learns several facts about crustaceans.

*　　*　　*

I knew both Michael and Nick really liked me, but in those days you didn't pay the kind of attention to this that you do now. Everyone hadn't been in psychotherapy, everyone wasn't so superaware of their own vulnerabilities and everybody else's. For all I know we didn't even use that word, vulnerability. Though I have to say I think we were more decent in other ways. But in terms of personal relationships, everything was very foggy. Maybe I just assumed other people didn't suffer the way I do.

Well, it's stupid trying to explain the dynamics of this kind of thing in the present. The point was that it followed the rules of another time, when such ambiguous arrangements were not uncommon and not questioned.

I guess I also thought they didn't like me *that* much. I mean, nothing was ever said or anything. And they both had things with other people, which, if I remember well, I somewhat resented. They had these girlfriends, now and then, both of them. They were cute girls, some of them, though for the most part they bored me. None of them was that long-lasting, anyway, because when you're on the road a lot, these things don't tend to have much substance that has enduring meaning. And we were on the road all the time, those days. But, anyway, it's not as if I had an exclusive on either of them or anything.

Plus, right from the start, in our last year of high school, I'd gone to bed with both of them. I mean, not together, though sometimes I might have liked to, of course, but it wasn't their thing. But I'd first had a thing with Nick, when we were kids, and then with Michael. I mean, before we had a group or anything. In fact, I'm not absolutely sure we would have had a group otherwise. They were sort of friendly before all this, but not really close. They were both too isolated. I guess I liked both of them so much I wanted to be together with both of them. So we used to smoke a lot of dope together and hang out and fool around with guitars. That was it, that was how it started. And for a long time I didn't go to bed again with either of them. I was busy sowing other oats elsewhere. And maybe also because I knew they both liked me and I didn't want to mess with that. I don't know. It was complicated. For instance, they both really liked each other too, but I was the one who enabled them to be friends.

Anyway, later, when we had the group, our lives became so chaotic that a lot of distinctions disappeared. Once we were on the road I slept with one or the other again, now and again. I have to tell you I don't exactly remember anymore. And then I'd feel like I had my fill of both of them and not be interested at all for a long time. Sometimes they just irritated me. I guess more and more as time went by. And maybe I irritated them too. And then I'd start up again. I know it seems ridiculous, but as I say, all of this seemed pretty foggy at the time. And nothing was ever said about it. Not one word. I mean, it would have been totally out of the question for either of them ever to admit to feeling any sexual jealousy.

And in the spirit of the times, everybody pretended sex wasn't such a big deal. Why am I saying "pretend"? Maybe it wasn't such a big deal. Oh, I don't know anymore. It's really, truly impossible to reconstruct now. And, you know, I could dress it up and make it seem nicer, and tidier, but the hell with that. I'd rather think of it just as it was. I'm not going to start pretending I was anything else, that I'm anything else than what I am. Fuck that shit. I've got enough troubles.

I'm not sorry for anything I've ever done. No regrets. Nothing.

Oh, Jesus I am *filled* with regrets.

I never knew how either of them really felt about all this. It's incredible, but I didn't. We never talked about it. Never. Still haven't ever.

I don't understand what happened. I still don't understand and I still don't know how much it had to do with me, or with anything. I swear I don't.

At the end of the first tour, we wound up in Boston, the ——— hotel. What a dump. We had a break of a couple of weeks, before we were supposed to go to New York to make our second album. Everybody else went home to rest. We were all really wasted. Michael and Nick and I decided to stay on. We were thinking of maybe going to the Cape though it was still early spring, too cold to swim. We were in a weird state. I guess we were crashing from the tour. The three of us must have been really crazy. That first night we all three of us just slept about twenty hours. We went to sleep the night before and then we met in the coffee shop at about eight o'clock the next night and had breakfast. So then we had some coffee and of course we felt completely wired, so then we decided to drive to the Cape that night and take the ferry to Martha's Vineyard, where we'd all been before. I don't know why we picked the Vineyard.

We were in a great mood in the car on the way down. We had just overnight bags and guitars and plenty of marijuana along with what Nick announced was a drug miscellany of unparalleled diversity, hallucinogenics, ups and downs. "Let's get smashed immediately," Nick had suggested. But after some discussion we decided to just get high on grass and save the rest of the stuff for the beach.

We kept the radio on and were singing along, just like kids. We felt we'd been freed from jail or something. I remember, just as we neared the coast, it got really sunny, and there was a Lovin' Spoonful record on the radio. "What a Day for a Daydream," we all sang along.

We checked into an inn, and each got our own rooms, which was a tremendous luxury to us. In fact we were blowing our wad, what with the car and the rooms.

Maybe it was at dinner that night that something happened

91

between Michael and me. I can't remember really how it started. It's hard to know how these things start. You don't really notice them until they're past the point where you can control them. But it was like this intensity between the two of us. I mean, it was really weird, because in the car on the way down, there'd been nothing. We were just having a really good time, the three of us together, and all of a sudden at dinner, we had some drinks or something and it was just different, there was that strange shimmer that happens between two people, that's almost imperceptible, that you feel almost more than you observe it.

It's really strange how a very powerful thing can be going on between two people and it's absolutely undistinguishable by the third. It happens, I think, with tiny movements of the eyes and a discernment through some exquisite magnification of the senses of the other person's behavior, just as if you have a telescope and no one else in the room does. I don't think Nick knew anything that night. It was too subtle. Even I couldn't know absolutely for sure.

I can't remember now, to tell you the truth, I can't remember for sure whether I actually registered what was going on. I was so vague in those days, and lagged so much in the tempest of events in my life. But I remember the way I felt, whether I acknowledged it to myself at the time or not, which is that weird spin that such an attraction puts on everything.

I don't know. It may also have been that I'd finally gotten some rest after being so exhausted.

The funny thing about that night was, I really didn't mind Nick being there. I liked it, actually. It seemed to me just like the earliest days when it was just the three of us fooling around. My goodness, I was already nostalgic. But, anyway, maybe that was part of the lightness of that evening too. We could act ourselves, or rather like whatever we thought "ourselves" were, if we still had selves, which is open to speculation, considering everything that had happened to us already.

Anyway, so I also felt this curious feeling of protection precisely because both of them were there. And there was among the three of us a strange sense of well-being, just sitting there in the corny dining room of that corny inn, with no responsibilities, with nowhere to go and no one to bother us.

It's weird because whenever I think of those few days it's usually with horror, but actually when I think of just that night, it was one of the best nights I ever had. It felt so safe. The thing between Michael and me, it didn't seem like a betrayal of Nick, it really didn't. It just felt like a little extra warmth, which in a curious way Nick was part of.

After dinner, we all went up to Nick's room, which had twin beds, so Nick sat down on his bed over by the window, and Michael sat down on a chair, and I lay down on the bed by the wall. Michael's guitar was in the room and of course he was sort of idly picking the strings, since in those days he couldn't sit down for any amount of time without playing. Then Nick took out some hashish and Michael moved over to the bed I was lying on. We used a pin and a pen top.

Michael remained on the bed I was lying on. He was sitting there with his back leaning against the wall so his back touched one of my legs a little, because I was behind him. I can't remember what we talked about, it just seems now to me like hashish conversation, but I still remember the way it felt, just those few inches of contact of his back, through his shirt, against my thigh, through my jeans.

The funny thing is, now that I think of it, that Michael and I were happy, and we made Nick happy too.

I fell asleep for a while, to the sound of their voices, and then woke up because Michael had his hand on my shoulder and was saying, Casey, do you want to go to bed? So I said okay. And we left the room. I was still sort of asleep. I opened the door to my own room and turned around and Michael sort of stood there for a minute and I wondered whether he was going to come into my room or not but he didn't move, so I said goodnight and he did too and I went into my room and closed the door.

To tell you the truth, I think that's what fucked everything up, was that particular moment. I didn't think about it too much that night. I mean, I did, but I was full of the feeling I had and which I'd actively felt that night, and of the smell of Michael

93

sitting next to me on that bed, and of the softness in his eyes. I lay in bed for a little while in this weird happy hash spin and felt sort of, sort of perfect, you know.

But the next morning when I woke up I kept thinking about that moment in the hall, and I thought maybe I'd imagined the whole thing, I mean that I'd imagined that there was something between Michael and me all evening. I thought, if there had been, he would have come into my room with me. I figured I'd imagined it, and that the hash had distorted my judgment, and that in the hall, when I turned around, he must have seen that I wanted him to come into my room and that what had happened was a rejection pure and simple. I kept playing that moment in my mind and the more I did, the more I saw his carefully neutral expression, the more I felt humiliated.

I went down to breakfast and Nick and Michael were sitting out on this glass veranda and they weren't saying anything, and by then I was in such a state of paranoia that I figured they hated me. Something had happened, in reaction to the night before or something, and everything seemed to me to be very tense and awful. At the same time, I wasn't sure. I mean, I knew the whole time that in fact perhaps the reason Michael hadn't come into my room the night before was because *I* hadn't invited him, I knew that the boys might just be sitting there in their habitual neutral mien because they were waiting for me to make a commitment of one mood or another that morning, but I was too paranoid to act on any such theories. Instead I became more and more anxious.

What never occurred to me at the time was that maybe the reason both of us had hesitated and had not been able to overcome our hesitation was because of Nick, still lying down in his hashish cloud in the room we had just left, and that there would have been something cruel, in the abstract, even if he hadn't known, about coming out of his room and going into mine together. I mean, on that particular night. Because we were no longer on the road or anything. It was just the three of us.

Instead, I started hating Nick, sitting there at that breakfast table. It was amazing, I just started detesting the way he ate and his hands and his hair which was as usual, uncombed. I went into this intense rage. And meanwhile this, I don't know, this warmth I'd felt for Michael the night before, was transformed into a fierce, raging lust. I went into some state of madness, I can't even decribe it now, sitting with those two boys and feeling this raging hate for one and lust for the other and it seemed to me at that breakfast that I was imploding, all the while we three sat there mute and drank coffee.

Michael's expression was, I guess you'd call it guarded. But then it always was. Nick, it was clear, was completely natural, or as natural as any of us got, in his usual self-conscious way.

It was nothing that unusual, you understand. Maybe that grim breakfast was also like when we'd be on stage with everything exploding but our faces cool and stern, or sitting in those dismal bars after a show looking bored and maybe a little restless but in truth still so psyched up that we barely knew what to do with ourselves. We were sort of used to compensating for one extreme with another, so it could all pass. The weirdest sort of behavior could pass just because your facial expression announced, in case anyone checked it out, that all this was no big deal.

We made some desultory small talk making fun of the room and the waitress and then, it was Nick, I think, Nick suggested we go to the beach.

If you'd seen us there that day at the beach, you would have seen nothing. I've been thinking of what happened that day for the last fifteen years, and I've never been able to decide what happened, if anything happened. If anything happened it was in the very slight inconsistency between words and gestures, in the air, some texts behind the texts behind the expressions. I was so upset, you see, over that moment the night before. It's taken me a very long time to even admit that something in my behavior could have revealed what I was really feeling, especially since I don't think I really understood what I was truly feeling, and at any rate that day I don't think that even I was truly aware of my behavior, and what was that behavior, anyway? I'm not sure, even now. Except that I didn't want Nick there. It's funny because all these years later I can't imagine how I could have shown that. Did I show it or not? Maybe I didn't. Maybe I didn't and I have no way to know. But what I'm trying to say is odd about it is that I didn't even fully acknowledge to myself that I didn't want Nick there, so how could he know?

I don't know, but Michael knew. I mean, with that eerie intuition people who are attracted to each other have. The thing is I was so upset about what had happened the night before, I was seized, I was obsessed with it, I was interested only in studying the hieroglyphs of body language, to see if I really had been rejected or if I was desired. This preoccupied me so much that the motions of life I was making on the beach that day were those of an actress. It didn't matter what was said or wasn't, which way we walked.

All the while, it was a beautiful day. A chilly spring day, but sunny, the kind that gives you a kind of anxious vitality. Scary but refreshing. You breathe deep and are conscious of wanting to be alive. Not a feeling we often had.

Anyway, here's what happened, here's all that happened: at one point, I walked away from Michael and Nick and went and sat down on a rock, and I waited. I waited for Michael. It was a test. But then it was Nick who strolled over. He just stood there a moment by the rock and said nothing. But then that's Nick typically, he wouldn't have said anything until I addressed him. I said nothing too. Nick stood there for a while and finally ambled away, without a glance.

I sat on the rock for a long time before Michael finally walked over. I was willing him to come over. That's all I wanted, I was like just reduced to this desire of having him walk over. If he'd come over right away, I probably would have given away nothing. I really think so, according to the rules by which we played, we might have exchanged a few words, maybe not, but I would have kept my gaze on the ocean. But I sat there on that rock for so long, reduced to only want, that I was broken. Watched the wind in the dunes and in the trees and in the waves and hated them and hated myself for wanting so much and was broken so that when finally, after I'd given up, Michael walked over, I looked up at him and my face must have been naked, and he looked back at me, just kept looking, so then I knew.

So that's all that happened. Michael sat down in the sand about a foot away. Another twenty feet away, Nick was sitting on the sand too, hugging his knees, staring out at the ocean.

Had he turned around, or had he seen, out of the corner of his eye, Michael and me just looking into each other's eyes for that instant too long?

That night after dinner I said I was tired and was going to bed. As I walked out of the room I heard Michael tell Nick that he was thinking of going on a walk, did Nick want to go for a walk. But I didn't hear the answer, and have never known if they went for a walk together that night. I went to my room and got undressed and turned off the light and went to bed and soon Michael came in and I heard the brushing of his clothes and I held the covers open and he came into my bed and I held my arms to him.

It's funny, all these years, I've often thought of that afternoon on the beach, every moment of it, I could describe every moment of it down to the smallest detail, but I'd forgotten until now that moment when Michael came into my bed that night and the sweetness of his body.

I don't know how much later it was that night that we heard Nick's step in the hall and stopped whispering. There was a knock at the door and we lay there silent. A minute went by, maybe, and there was another knock, and we lay there hearing the sound of our own breath. Then we heard Nick walk away and for a little while we continued to lie there silent and still. Then Michael put his hand on my head, under my hair and I could feel him just feeling the shape of my head, the way somebody does when they love you and they want to know of what you are composed, what is the shape of the substance they love. Then he kissed me again.

I was asleep when he left the room. I was asleep the next morning when he shook my shoulder. He was dressed. He sat on the edge of the bed and I put my hand on his knee and now I remember the feeling of his jeans under my fingers. But I opened my eyes and I saw he looked pale and tired.

"I've brought you some coffee," he said, pointing to a Styrofoam cup on the night table.

"What's the matter?" I said.

He only said my name. "Casey," he said, very gently.

It gave me this shooting sensation in my belly. I wanted to make love with him again. Just looking at him. Michael was one of those boys you make love with and then want to make love with again. I'd always forget, in between. There are some people you only want to fuck once. You know how sometimes you go to bed with someone and it can be fine but then whatever it was that sparked between you is consummated? It's not that you possess them but that you now possess the thing that was between you, so you're not hungry for it anymore. And then some guys, you make love with them and you just can't get enough and you want more and more and more and more.

I put my hand on his cheek but his expression didn't change. I thought he looked that way because he loved me. Maybe that's what it was.

"What's the matter?" I asked. "What happened?" He said nothing and I suddenly realized the reason he wasn't saying anything was that he couldn't talk. I sat up. "What happened? What happened?" I repeated, like an idiot.

Nick had taken so much stuff it was hard to say exactly what killed him. It was hard to say whether he'd meant to kill himself or whether he'd wanted to get truly smashed, as he would have put it. The autopsy was inconclusive. Everything was inconclusive.

Ken flew up that day and he and Michael took care of everything. Or maybe he took care of everything and Michael stayed in his room as I did in mine. The next morning, all of us flew back to New York, we three in the passenger seats and Nick's body somewhere else in the plane, in a plastic bag.

In a plastic bag. In a fucking green plastic bag.

"What happened? Did anything happen?" Ken kept asking.

And we both kept saying no. What was I going to tell him? About that moment on the beach when Michael and I looked at each other an instant too long? I mean, to this day, I don't know if Nick even looked up. It wouldn't have been like him to look up. But then I remember the three of us, me on my rock and Michael a foot or so away and then a space on the beach and then Nick sitting on his rock hugging his knees and that picture tells me that Nick knew. He had to know.

And that knock. That knock on the door. Oh my God, how many nights in all these years have I lain awake in some dump and thought of Nick on the other side of that door. And did he know Michael was with me? He knocked twice. I can't believe he would have waited and then knocked again if he'd known we were together.

But so what, you might say. I mean, was that sufficient cause for anything?

No, of course not. I mean, I don't know what happened that day. I just know that the last time Michael and I were in some sort of ambiguous triangle somebody got wiped out.

Oh, I'm not stupid. You think I don't know what's going on? I'm not that stupid anymore.

*   *   *

part
2

SOMETIMES, AFTER DINNER, CASEY, MICHAEL AND LESLIE GO AND SIT outside and look out at the ocean. Michael and Leslie's house, unlike the one Casey has rented, is not on a beach but on a ridge about fifty feet above the ocean. It's Leslie who likes going and sitting out there. It's to make Leslie happy. Michael checks to make sure that Sebastian has fallen asleep, and that his window is open so that they'll hear him if he calls out. Then they trek out to a round wooden table in front of the house, carrying mugs of tea, a plate of cookies, Casey's cigarettes and ashtray. They always choose the same seats, Leslie in the middle.

Until around the time of Casey's arrival, Michael and Leslie used to walk all the way out to the drop over the ocean, and, often, even clamber down to the little strip of sand and rock that is exposed when the tide is low, but now Leslie's declared that the slide down and the climb back up, in the dark, especially when there is no moon to see by, stumbling over roots and stones, is part of the growing category of activity that she is too pregnant to perform.

"But why don't you two go ahead?" says Leslie.

"Too scary," says Casey.

"It is quite terrifying, actually," says Michael.

"It really isn't dangerous," says Leslie. "The worst that can happen is you'll slide on the seat of your pants for a few feet, there are too many bushes to really fall."

"That's not what's terrifying," says Michael. "It's the violence of the ocean and the vastness of the dark sky."

"Mm," says Leslie. "Dee-lish."

"Yeah," says Casey. "I'm even scared up here."

Michael and Leslie laugh at Casey's delivery.

"No kidding," says Casey. "That *sound!*"

"I love that," says Leslie. "I find it pacifying." She puts her hand on her belly. "I'm sure it's good for the baby to hear it."

"You think they can hear?" says Casey.

"I think he must at least sense it," says Leslie.

"Maybe I should play this baby some Leadbelly," says Michael. "So he could start out sensing some good blues."

"I'd start him on Robert Johnson," says Casey. "He can work his way to Leadbelly."

"Are you making fun of me?" asks Leslie good-naturedly.

Michael turns to Leslie and takes her hand.

It's the first time Casey has seen Michael touch Leslie. Casey swivels away, lights a cigarette, puts it down in the ashtray, digs in her pocket for a rubber band, and pulls her hair into a ponytail. When she settles back in her chair again, Michael has put his hands back in his pockets and is leaning back, his chair tilted onto its back legs. Leslie turns to Casey and smiles at her and tugs at her ponytail a bit. Casey smiles back.

"I'm still hungry," says Michael, who has missed the silent exchange between the two women.

"Maybe we should have some ice cream," says Leslie.

"Yeah, okay," says Michael. "What kind?"

"I'm not sure what there is," says Leslie. "I'll go see."

"No, no, I'll go," says Casey, and rises before Leslie can move.

Casey turns on the light in the kitchen and blinks a bit and rubs her face.

"Well, fuck *me*," she says out loud. She puts her hand on her chest.

When she comes back out again she is carrying a tray with two bowls of ice cream and a small glass of vodka.

"I've got to go soon," she says, after sitting down and taking a sip of the vodka.

"Really?" says Leslie. "Already?"

"Don't go yet," says Michael. "Not just yet."

*   *   *

The joke was on me, but I got better as a singer after Nick died. Even though we felt pretty much destroyed, each in our own way, the group had enough momentum so there was no question by then of disbanding. We didn't even interrupt our schedule. It became clear, as unbelievable and humorous as it seemed to us, that Ex-Lovers was going to make it, and that if we really went for it we might make it pretty big. There was no time to stop for anything, death or birth or depression or anything in those days. We were due in the studio in a few weeks and in we went.

We didn't talk about it, Nick's death, except about the press who were hanging around outside the studio like vultures. Naturally, they loved that story, the three of us in this godforsaken inn, sex, death and rock 'n' roll, what more could they ask for, those scavengers. Michael and I never talked about it, to this day. I didn't see him after that plane ride until we got back into the studio, and then we were nervous with one another, and I guess for a while we almost avoided each other.

The whole dynamic of the group changed in fact. A band isn't just a modular assembly of musicians. Its personality and its sound can really change with even just one different musician. So we got a new bass player, Jim Blunt. He was good too, better than Nick, I guess, though it took me a long time to get used to it. He was a big guy and played real steady. It wasn't as delicate and cool as the way Nick used to play, but it was strong and funky. It was pretty cool in its own way, actually, though at the time I sort of hated to listen to the bass part. For a long time it sort of hurt me to listen to the bass part. Pretty stupid, I suppose. He was okay, Jim Blunt, a real good-looking guy, hip on stage, kind of scrungy, which was appealing at the time.

Well, but anyway, everything sort of changed, because this guy was fine, but we didn't, at least Michael and I, become really good friends with him. I think up to that point the band had been like a family, so that for example, when Will came in we'd become really good friends with him, even though he was someone we'd never really talk to if we'd met him under other circumstances. But no one could really replace Nick for us and as much as we liked this new guy we couldn't help resenting him on some level. And, besides, when somebody you love dies, you start protecting yourself more, start avoiding getting close to people so you won't be so hurt when they leave, one way or another, and it's just as well I did that because I certainly have been left a lot since then, been died on a whole bunch of times, oh my God, when I think about it it seems to me that my whole story is just a story of everything dying, everyone dying, one way or another, though maybe it's just their youth that dies and maybe if you do what I do there's just nothing sadder than your youth dying.

Well, so maybe, now that I think of it, maybe all this had the effect of making me harder. I mean, I had to protect myself and I grew some calluses. Like a carapace. I felt isolated so I became tougher, the whole operation became more businesslike, and then these things have a way of gathering momentum.

The odd thing was, maybe lucky for me, maybe not, that I did start to sing differently. It was because of the state I was in when we went in to do that album. In a way, I no longer gave a shit. I got through laying down the tracks in a kind of daze. Will and Michael really took care of everything, which I guess set the pattern for what came later in terms of producing the records. Will and Michael took care of everything and I just got through the nights. Then when it came time to do my vocals I just . . . I don't know. I guess I was desperate, I sang like I was desperate, and there was something that worked about it, musically.

I started keeping a bottle in the studio and drinking a little, which I'd never done before. I used to drink a little before going on stage but not in the studio because I used to be too worried about singing in tune, but I stopped worrying about that when we made that record and I started wailing much more and somehow the pitch was always what it should have been once I became less self-conscious.

"You're sounding great, Casey," everyone kept saying to me, and Ken was like practically rubbing his hands, that bastard, he was just in the best mood because he knew we were making hits in there and he was probably thinking if Nick hadn't died he ought to have killed him to get that sound we got when we all became so much looser.

It's pretty ugly, isn't it? When I think back, now, it seems pretty ugly to me.

The worst night was the night we did the vocals on a song Nick had written, which we'd decided to keep on the new record. And, naturally, of all the songs we did for that record, that one came easiest. Life's always just too corny, isn't it? There've been some mighty hokey songs written—I know, I've sung a lot of them—but there's never been a song hokeyer than real life.

It was a blues, Nick's song, and we'd laid down a really solid, soulful track on it. And that night I was psyched up just right, or had just the right amount to drink, or whatever the fuck, I don't know, but for the one and only time before or since, I did the song in one take. I don't know, I just went into some kind of weird space, a weird dark space where there was nothing but my voice, and it was as if I didn't have to make any effort to produce it, or worry about pitch or rhythm, or anything. It was like a serpent coming out of me, as if that's what had been in my chest, this column of pain, and I could just hurtle it out of my throat in the form of a blues. I never forgot that feeling and the state I was in to produce it, and I was able to do it again later, and on stage, though it isn't a reliable thing, but I can do it pretty often with a certain kind of tune.

But that night was when I found that state which I didn't even know existed, that place. I didn't even know yet that you could do it on purpose or anything. I just sang, and we didn't stop and start

107

the way we always did because I'd heard something that bothered me or whatever, we kept going, and then we played it back and everyone knew we couldn't get a better performance than that one.

I was upset afterward. Michael was upset too, I could see. We all went out to dinner, and I drank more than usual, which was saying a lot at that particular point, to try to calm myself down, and after a while the liquor started to ease that raw thing in me left where the serpent had been, but every once in a while, I'd look across the table where Michael was and I could see he was upset and it reawakened this pain. So, I don't know, at a certain point, everybody wasn't even finished eating yet, but I looked across the table at Jim Blunt, who was sitting next to Michael, and I said, "Hey, Jim!" and he looked up, and I said, "Do you want to hit the sack with me?" and I remember that table suddenly seemed like a stage set because everyone became quiet, it was atrocious, and Michael's face, next to Jim's, Michael's face looking absolutely blank, and Jim Blunt smiled and said, "Now, you mean?" "Sure, now," I said, and in a way, it was like being back in the studio, because my voice was coming out of me without any volition on my part. "Ready?" I said, and Jim stood up, and I did too and we walked out of the restaurant.

A few months later, Jim crashed his motorcycle into some wall or some post, and lost a leg. Fucked himself up pretty bad. He couldn't play anymore. We had to get yet another new bass player for our third album. Will and Ken started making jokes about it.

It was a joke, I guess. Seems like a joke now to a lot of people. Not long ago I saw a tape of this movie, *Spinal Tap*, and I thought, shit, I've become a joke. In the movie, the drummers kept dying. They kept having to replace the drummers.

Well, maybe that's better. I'd rather think of it as a joke, because I can't bear to think of all the people I loved, even for just one night, who are dead or wasted. It's better as a joke, believe me. I can't even think about it, as a rule. I have to really be willing to get fucked up to let myself think about it.

*   *   *

Sometimes Michael and Leslie bring Sebastian to Casey's house, because the little boy loves to swim in the pool. The three adults station themselves at regular intervals in the pool and the four-year-old splashes his way from one to the other with unrestrained and indefatigable delight. Finally, it's Michael or Leslie who must announce the time has come for lunch and Sebastian, complaining, is fed and taken to Casey's bedroom for a nap. Sebastian has become fiercely enamored of Casey and always insists on a song, as a condition for a nap. When the song ends, Leslie is there to insist that there will be no other and to convince Sebastian that to take a nap now will bring closer the moment when he can go back in the pool for another swim.

But in the last few days, Sebastian has become obstreperous and needy, and today he has a tantrum, right in the middle of lunch, and won't be talked into calming down. Michael sits Sebastian on his lap but the little boy keeps whimpering and struggling to get loose.

"Maybe I should take him home," says Michael.

"No," says Leslie. "I will. I think I'm probably as wiped out as he is."

"You know, I can fend for myself," says Casey, "if you guys want to split. I can just meet up with you later."

"No," says Leslie. "It's been like this all week, and I think Michael could use a break."

With Lesie and Sebastian gone, it's very quiet.

"Are you upset?" Casey asks Michael.

"It's pretty upsetting. Although there isn't anything that can

109

be done. I think he's nervous with Leslie so pregnant and with the idea of a usurper coming into the world in another month. And maybe I've been weird too."

"Have you?" says Casey. She pauses, a shrimp midway to her mouth. Michael looks at her.

"Am I disruptive here?" she says.

"Casey, you're so paranoid," said Michael. "I always thought it was one of your great charms."

"No, come on."

"Eat your shrimp," says Michael.

Casey puts the shrimp back down on her plate.

"Listen," she begins, but stops when Michael puts his napkin down and stands.

She remains silent as he walks over to the picture window and looks out at the ocean. It's a slightly overcast afternoon, the air is very slightly gray and very slightly violet. In the room, the light is delicate. Michael walks over to an armchair facing the ocean and sits down. Casey, at the table, can't see his face.

"Yes, of course, you're disruptive," says Michael. "If you mean does your being here bring up some memories that are painful, or if it reminds me that maybe there are some things I should be doing that I'm not."

"I didn't mean . . ." says Casey. "I'm sorry. I didn't mean to . . ."

"No, what I'm saying," says Michael, "is that it's not a bad thing."

"I don't know," says Casey, "I mean we haven't really been talking about anything, I haven't known what to . . . I mean, I don't know."

"No, we haven't really talked very much, in a serious way or anything, but then I guess I'm not very good at talking about anything in a serious way. It just occurred to me now to try."

"Well, the thing is," says Casey, "I meant . . ." Then she stops again.

"If you meant that it's disruptive to have you here because of the feelings I have about you, well, no, it isn't," says Michael. "I mean, it is but it isn't. I'm not really sure, anyway, of what feelings I have about you."

Casey exhales. "Me neither," she says. "I thought . . . I thought maybe that's why I should leave."

"Well, I guess I wish you wouldn't," says Michael. "I mean, I think you're in trouble, or you have been in trouble, and that you've been better since you've been here, which means I've been able to help you a little."

"Oh, you've helped me a lot," Casey interrupts, on easy ground now.

"Because I never used to be able to," he says. "I always wanted to, I could always see you needed help, but I didn't even know how to begin."

"No, you're different now," says Casey.

"I've learned a lot from Leslie," says Michael. "Maybe because I didn't expect to. But I guess because of the way things happened or the state I was in, I trusted Leslie and she helped me, so then I saw how it was done. I mean, I saw how it was possible to be friends. That is, to make some kind of human contact and everything or, say, to call it what most people call it, to love someone."

Casey says nothing. A vein throbs in her temple. "Where are my sunglasses?" she says.

"Here," says Michael.

"Ah," says Casey. She puts them on.

"Great shades," says Michael.

"Thanks," she says.

"If you mean," continues Michael, "that there's some kind of thing between us, something between the lines somehow, well, yes, there is, of course. Is that disruptive?"

"You're really brave," says Casey. "I didn't think you were capable of being that honest."

"Well," he says. "Me neither. But what I'm trying to say is, it's not necessarily a bad thing. I mean, we don't have to do anything about it. It'll go away. I'm willing to just let it sit there for a while and maybe talking about it like this will help it go away, and it's worth trying."

"Okay," says Casey. "I think it's worth trying."

"Or," says Michael, "do you think this is all bullshit?"

"I don't know," says Casey. "No. I don't think it's bullshit."

"Let's try to be friends, okay?" says Michael. "I could use a friend."

"Me too," says Casey. "I really, really could. I haven't had a friend in a really long time."

*   *   *

Well, I don't know. What a mess. Or is it a mess? What were my motives, anyway, in asking if I was disruptive? Was I being considerate or did I want to try and provoke precisely the reaction I got, and which I wanted? And did I want it?

Yes. I mean let's not kid ourselves. I wanted him to say there was some kind of thing between us. The air became charged with heavier ions once he said that, it gave me a feeling of . . . I don't know what to call it. Happiness. Maybe that feeling is called happiness.

Or maybe it was just a thrill. I hate that word, happiness. What is the difference between a moment of happiness and a thrill? Is there a difference?

I don't know. I'm fucked up. I feel really fucked up this morning. Too agitated. I'd gotten much better lately, but this morning the hellhound is back on my trail. Or have I really gotten better? Am I ever going to get better?

Sure. All right. Tote that barge.

I, actually, for the first time in a long time, wish I had a piano. I guess I've got a little negative energy to discharge. Maybe it gets stored up from not playing the piano. Maybe I should rent a piano. Maybe I should split. Should I split?

The thing that plagues me is, does Leslie know? No, Leslie can't know. I barely knew. I barely know.

I mean, nothing happened. Some words were said, is all. Maybe I'm making too big a thing of this. I'm just stranded on this island. If we were anywhere else, it wouldn't be such a big deal at all. Anyway, I don't think it was such a bad thing for me to provoke a conversation, because it'll clear the air. It was the right thing to do.

I can't leave. I cannot face New York right now. Hell, I'm just barely keeping myself together here, how am I going to face all those jokers back there? How am I going to face myself back there? To say nothing of Anthony. I've got to call back Anthony and I don't know what to tell him. I've got to tell him something.

The thing is, that feeling I had yesterday, when Michael was talking to me. It was so powerful, it sort of left me inarticulate. And I know, in my heart I know, I shouldn't have had that feeling, and I shouldn't be nursing it now. I mean, this is nothing but trouble. Nothing but heartache can come of this, and I better start watching my step, right now. It's so odd. I was so unprepared. I just hadn't had that feeling in such a long time. Plus, it just seems too ridiculous that I should feel this way about Michael, because Michael and me is such an old story. I would have figured you have something like that with someone and then when you consummate it you use it up. Although I guess in a way this is exactly what happened at Martha's Vineyard. I mean, I got faked out that time too. I also thought at the time that it couldn't happen, that it was used up.

Well, but I was so stupid then. I was so young and stupid.

And how did he know what I felt? And if he knew, maybe Leslie knows. He must have known, to say what he said, he must have known how I felt, and how did he know? Did I give myself away by what I said or how I looked? Man, I have got to cool it.

The thing is, though, I knew. I mean I knew he had these feelings about me, and I wasn't completely surfacing on that. Partly because I was afraid I was wrong. And maybe I wasn't even surfacing on my own feelings about it really because I was afraid he didn't feel that way and it's too lonely feeling that way by myself. Anyway, the thing is, did I know all along? I mean, was my coming to this island in the first place pretty suspect?

Oh, this is ridiculous. Fucking ridiculous, man.

The sea's pretty choppy today. Maybe that's my problem. Maybe I'm magnifying all this stuff way out of proportion and I'm just upset because there's a storm coming. It's funny, I know there's a storm coming. I really wouldn't have thought I could be in the slightest bit in tune with nature, I've been inside so long.

I've been inside so long would make a good line for something. Maybe I should try to work. Maybe I should rent a piano here and try to do something here.

Maybe I should go for a run. I don't feel like running today. I feel like lying here like a invalid staring at the ocean, is what I feel like doing. I wish I could stop thinking about this conversation yesterday. It's funny, that ocean was just a big blue stretch to me when I first got here and now it seems to me as if it has something to say to me every day. Every day it has a different song to sing, a song I hear. Maybe the song the ocean sings is the song I sing too. Maybe that's how everything works.

I wonder if I can still write any good songs. I don't have anything new to say, really. I don't have anything to say at all I haven't said a thousand times already.

Sometimes I look at this here ocean and I try to remember how the ocean was that day at the beach with Michael and Nick. It's weird, because I remember the beach so clearly, but I can't remember what the sea was like. Was it calm even? It was different from this blue-green sea, I rememer that. I think it was grayish, sort of. I don't know, I was turned so inward.

That night, on Martha's Vineyard, when we went to bed, Michael talked to me. He said my name. I mean, I remember it because he never had before. It wasn't while we were fucking, but afterward, I was lying close to him, and we were both wet with sweat and semen and I had this burst of tenderness for him or something, I don't know, I slid closer to him and put my arms around him and he just said "Casey."

I could hear the ocean, I do remember that, lying in that little room in the little rickety inn, and he said "Casey," and then I listened for more, but there was just the sound of the sea.

The sea is sort of like what an audience sounds like sometimes. Like the sea, you can't tell if it's pleased or angry.

Maybe I should get a piano here.

*   *   *

115

"I called my friend Anthony," Casey tells Leslie, "and he's going to come and visit me."

The two women are sitting at the wooden table in front of Michael and Leslie's house, finishing lunch. Michael is in town. Sebastian is playing on the grass a few feet away.

"Really?" says Leslie. "The guy you were living with in New York?"

"Well, I wasn't really living with him," says Casey. "He was my lover."

"I've never really had a lover," says Leslie.

Casey laughs. "It's a stupid word. Is that what you mean?"

Leslie tilts her head upward in a way she has when she's thinking about something and squints a little in the sun. "Well, no," she says. "I mean, when I was a kid, I had boyfriends. Then I was always living with someone, which doesn't count as a lover."

"Well, it can," says Casey.

"No," says Leslie. "I always like that word because I think it refers to a certain kind of love, which maybe you take for granted because a lot of people must love you this way, like lovers. I mean when they love you whether you love them or not. I bet you've had many lovers. I mean, aside from the real ones."

"Fans," says Casey, "are not lovers."

"But aren't they in a way?" asks Leslie. "I mean, because they desire you without conditions."

"But it's one-sided," says Casey. "Though of course in a way it isn't."

116

"But the unconditional thing . . ."

"Well!" expostulates Casey. "If a lover is someone who desires you unconditionally, then I've never had one either. Certainly not Anthony, who is the kind of person who never gets up in the morning without a dozen conditions."

"Really?" says Leslie. "Like what?"

"Oh," says Casey, "for the world to be more civilized. Of course, his conditions are never met, so he's caustic for the rest of the day, every day."

"That's funny," says Leslie. "When you said conditions I thought you meant he has conditions he expects from you in the morning."

"Oh, certainly not!" says Casey in a mock-indignant way. "He wouldn't presume."

"I have to bring Michael his breakfast in bed every morning," says Leslie.

"You do?" says Casey. "That's an outrage."

"Otherwise he doesn't get up. I don't mind so much, actually, except he's often incredibly grumpy."

"A leftover," says Casey. "From the old days. We were forced to get up after not enough sleep for so many years I don't think any of us will ever feel we get enough."

"I can't believe how much he sleeps," says Leslie. "Every night he crashes like timber. Especially lately. I think he used to keep himself awake to make love, but now I can't have sex anymore."

"You can't?"

"No. Although it's funny, because for the first seven months, sex is actually great when you're pregnant. I mean, it's better."

"Really?" says Casey.

"They say it's because you have more blood in your vagina. And also, I don't know, I guess because of the way being pregnant makes you feel. But toward the end, you're too weird, and your body is too fucked up."

Casey surveys Leslie for a moment. "You don't look like your body is fucked up, though you look pretty huge. But I think it's kind of cool-looking."

"No," says Leslie. "You can't imagine. Like your ribs separate."

"Your ribs separate?" repeats Casey incredulously.

"Well, yes," says Leslie. "To make room, you know."

"God!" says Casey.

"Do you want some more tea?" asks Leslie.

"Yes," says Casey, "but I'll get it."

"I don't mind, actually," says Leslie. "I am starting to find it hard to move around. Although I'm also finding it hard to sit still. I'm kind of looking forward to this being over."

Casey walks into the kitchen and puts water on to boil. "Can you feel it moving?" she calls out to Leslie through the open window.

"Yes, like crazy," Leslie calls back. "Like a boy. He moves like a boy."

"A boy like me?" Sebastian yells out.

Both women laugh. Sebastian abandons his shovel and his carefully arranged pebbles, totters over to Leslie and puts his head on her lap.

"Yes, Sebastian, a boy like you and like Michael."

"More like me than Michael," says Sebastian. "Because he'll be little."

"But you can't absolutely count on it," says Leslie. "It could be a little girl."

"I hope not!" says Sebastian.

Leslie leans over Sebastian, and Casey, standing in the kitchen waiting for the water to boil, looks out at the two blond heads together, framed by palm trees and then, behind the drop, the ocean.

Casey pours the tea, sets the pot and the mugs on a tray and then calls out, "Who wants a cookie?"

"Me!" yells Sebastian. "Me!"

"Me too!" calls back Michael.

Casey sticks her head out the window.

"Hi!" she says.

"Hi," says Michael.

"I'll have a cookie too," says Leslie.

Casey, humming, puts the bag of cookies on the tray and comes out of the kitchen.

"Well," she says. "Me too. Cookies all around."

"What's new?" says Michael when Casey sits down.

"I think I'm going to rent a piano," says Casey.

"And her friend Anthony is coming to visit," says Leslie.

"The Anthony I met in New York?" says Michael.

"Yeah," says Leslie.

"He's coming to stay with you?"

"Well, yeah, I guess so. Sunday. I think he's coming on Sunday."

"Well," says Michael. "Certainly a lot of action around here."

"Certainly a lot of action around here," repeats Sebastian tripping over the words somewhat, but with the same solemn expression.

*　　*　　*

I think it was a good idea to ask Anthony to come here. He sounded okay on the phone. He's not going to give me a hard time. Anthony, actually, is too smooth to give me a hard time. I'd forgotten that. I don't know why I was so angry with him anyway. I think I was angry with myself and my problems and I got angry with him too, which wasn't really fair, since Anthony never promised me anything he didn't deliver. Of course, Anthony's never failed me, because he promised me nothing, which was exactly what I wanted. For one thing I really felt I was at the end of the road with men. Let's face it, it's never worked out. I was tired of pretending I still believed it could work out.

It wasn't just that, actually, maybe I was also attracted to precisely that in Anthony. Anthony gave up like, decades ago, on anything but living with a certain kind of style, the way only Europeans can, I think. Americans always have to keep hoping for something. Anyway, I think the whole world-weary bit wasn't just convenient for me, but it also attracted me, maybe because it was a classier version of what I felt or could act out at the time. Also, because I'd never had one of those.

But to tell you the truth, sometimes I wonder if living with a certain kind of style isn't the one really interesting thing to do. I mean, for instance, Anthony has this elaborate moral framework that interests me a lot. It seems to have something to do with world-weariness but, actually, it's very optimistic. I mean, Anthony takes it for granted that life has meaning.

Maybe I was flattered, too. I'd run into Anthony at a number of parties and jaded though I may have thought I was, I wasn't insensitive to the value of the conquest. I'd been told he was really smart and really funny but I didn't know much about him except that he used to look at me in a slightly wicked way that was very seductive. The night I decided to zero in on him, there were several women sort of hovering around him. I just looked at him and smiled and he excused himself to whichever woman he was talking to and walked over to me. It was very frank and that interested me.

And Anthony was completely cool about things like fame. I mean, he was just right. I knew I was a pretty valuable social bauble to him, but that didn't really offend me. I don't have all that many choices in that area. My public self always winds up being a character in any relationship I have. Sometimes I think it's a more active factor than my real character. I mean, there's a difference, though a lot of people don't know that or else maybe they know that but they forget, and I must admit that maybe sometimes I do too. I complain a lot about people reifying me, but maybe that's my fault too. Maybe I hide behind it. Or, at least, rest behind it. In any event, the way other women have children who are part of the package, I have this bundle of fame I can't rid myself of. But Anthony, who was accustomed to being in the company of famous people, and who has quite a bit of renown in his own field, seemed to genuinely handle it. And it was great for me, actually, that he was older, and knew very little about rock 'n' roll beyond the obvious, and I kind of liked that too. But besides, I think Anthony truly likes me.

His conversation is amusing, anyway. Oh, I don't know. I am just hoping it is going to cool me out, about Michael. Maybe I could cool out. I've got to.

I can't believe how much I like Leslie. I guess I never spend enough time anymore in a natural situation with anyone new so I can get to like them. It's been such a long time since I've had any women friends. Not that Leslie could really be my close pal; she's too young. But that's part of what I like about her. I mean, I can see all the things Michael really likes about her. Loves about her.

On the other hand, maybe there's something too good to be true about Leslie. Maybe she's just shallow. Or callow.

I can't imagine what it's like to live for a long time with someone you love. Does love get boring?

In a weird way, as much as they drove me crazy, the way I felt about the guys in the group is probably the closest I've come to staying faithful ever. I mean, in my mind. In fact, I didn't leave them, they left me, all of them. Although that's not fair, I guess. I mean, they didn't have much of a choice really. As it is, both Will and Michael probably stayed in the group longer than they should have. The truth is, none of us were meant to be in a rock 'n' roll group. It was okay when we were kids but it was ridiculous after a while, except for the songwriting, which I think continued to interest them, but it just wasn't possible to continue being essentially sidemen, despite the money and all the rest.

Me neither, really, but I got too big to stop, is what happened. I wonder if it would all have been different if I hadn't fronted the group. Sometimes I really wish it had gone differently, and maybe we'd have stayed together. I don't know, because at the same time, I don't know what else I'd have to live for. It turned out there was this thing I could do, and it saved me in many ways. That is, the life I had to live to do it wrecked me, but who knows what would have happened to me otherwise. Maybe it saved me.

I wish something would save me. I wish someone would save me. What the fuck am I doing? I can't even think straight.

What else does anyone live for? I once knew, I think. I remember having a sense of it. I don't know anymore. Staying alive just to be alive, is that all? It just can't be. It can't be. Not for me.

Oh my God, I've got it bad for Michael now. My God, it's bad. Oh, I've got it so bad so bad so bad.

Katherine Cora! my mother used to yell at me. *You're impossible! You're an impossible brat! You'll be punished one day!* But she was wrong. There's no punishment. Or rewards, for that matter. That would make too much sense. It just always stays impossible. You never figure out what possible means.

* * *

part
3

"Now these palm trees," says Anthony as they pull into Casey's driveway, "hold out a promise for hilarity. Why is it that palm trees seem like ideal props for low farce?"

"You're so vain, Anthony," says Casey.

"Me, vain?"

"Yes," she says.

"Of what?"

"I don't know how to put it," Casey says.

"Vain of my highly developed sensitivity to detail and its implication?"

She smiles. "Yes," she says. "Exactly."

"Well, I am a writer," he says.

"I never forget that," she says.

"Are you hostile or admiring?" asks Anthony.

Casey laughs. "Don't worry. Mainly admiring," she says. "It's just that I've been here for two months and I forgot it looks ridiculous."

Anthony looks at his watch. "My plane only landed half an hour ago. I think I should be granted at least one hour in which to find this place ridiculous."

"All right," says Casey.

"I do love," says Anthony, pointing through the windshield at their surroundings, "the recently weathered clapboard, the astonishingly blue pool, and the Lucite birdhouses. But most of all the palms."

"Okay, so it's pretty silly," she says. "I'm entertained. But don't be sarcastic when Leslie and Michael are around, because they've been wonderfully nice to me. I don't want to make them feel bad. But it's true, it's silly."

"It's surprisingly silly," he says. "It's living up to my most extravagant expectations."

"Are you sorry you came?" asks Casey.

"I'm delighted I came," says Anthony, sounding as serious as he ever gets. "And delighted to be in your company once more, my dear."

Casey laughs. "I've really missed your superciliousness," she says.

"I certainly hope so," says Anthony. "It's exactly what I meant you to do."

They get out of the car, Anthony in his tweeds and corduroys, Casey in her now customary shorts and halter, barefoot and tanned.

"Now that I see you I don't know what zone I'm in," she says to Anthony as they walk toward the house.

"Pardon?" he asks.

"Oh," she says. "It's hard to explain."

"Well, as soon as I'm settled," he says, "we'll have a drink and you can explain."

"Oh, I don't know," she says. "Forget it."

"Well, I see we haven't lost any of our perversity on the other side of the world."

"Sometimes I get tired of hearing myself talk," says Casey.

"That often happens to me," says Anthony. "Which, as you can imagine, is most inconvenient for a writer."

"Did you bring work to do?" asks Casey.

"Are you changing the subject?" asks Anthony.

They walk into the house. Casey stops and so Anthony does too, and puts down his suitcase. She turns to him and puts her hand on his shoulder. His eyes look amused and kind.

"I'm sorry," she says. "I feel a little crazy."

He smiles at her. "That's never detracted from your very considerable charms," he says.

Casey smiles back and then looks away and twists her mouth a little.

"Are you embarrassed?" he asks. "You always do that with your mouth when you're embarrassed."

She looks back into his eyes. "Just bear with me a little, okay?" she asks.

"That's not difficult," says Anthony.

Casey takes her hand down from his shoulder. "Okay!" she exclaims. "Let's begin your Pacific vacation. Do you want to change?"

He follows her down the hall.

"This is your room," says Casey, opening a door. There's the

126

visual assault of the ocean, oddly silent behind the thick plate of the picture window.

"It's simple," she says. "I hope it doesn't seem too sparse to you." It contains only a bed, facing the ocean, and a night table.

"It's my room?" asks Anthony, putting his suitcase down on the bed.

"Yes," says Casey. "Is it okay?"

"Where are you?" asks Anthony.

"Just down the hall," says Casey.

"Good," says Anthony.

Casey laughs. "Change and I'll make you a drink," she says.

Casey's own room is at the end of the house, a corner room with two picture windows. The room seems half beach and ocean. Casey stops in to check herself in a mirror. She smooths back her hair and stands looking at herself for a moment. Then she sits down on the bed. She sighs. "Hell," she says out loud.

*　　*　　*

I must look unbelievably strange to Anthony, in my ponytail and shorts. He's too tactful to mention it. In fact, come to think of it, I haven't spent much time lately looking at myself in mirrors. And God knows, that's a relief. I do look strange. I don't look like myself. It's kind of frightening, actually. It's impossible to know what Anthony thinks. Was it really a good idea to have him come?

I don't feel like myself. I feel far away from myself. So far away.

I can't stop thinking about Michael. I don't know what's happened to me in the last couple of days. Jesus Christ, it's unbearable. I can't stop. It's like he's on power rotation in my mind.

No matter what, I can't let Anthony know, not even suspect any of this. For one thing, it's possible he might be jealous. I don't know. He's never exhibited anything like jealousy, but also he might be angry and I can't risk it. I can't have any kind of a scene, I couldn't take it. But also, he'd think I'm ridiculous. Of course, I am ridiculous.

I can't believe I actually got myself into this situation of being alone in a house on an island with someone to whom I have to lie about every aspect of my consciousness.

Oh, maybe I don't have to lie. I can keep up whatever pretense I want, it doesn't matter. Anthony knows me. It doesn't matter what I say to him. I mean, I can lie to him and he does or he doesn't believe me and it doesn't really matter.

Oh my God I'm ill. Why can't I stop thinking about him? This is going to drive me crazy.

Right now I can look in the mirror and see him behind me. In this fading light I can configure some of the shadows in the room into Michael. I wish I could lie down and think of him, think of just him, but I guess that's why it's a good idea to have Anthony here. This way lies hell.

Get up, get up. But I see Michael behind me looking at me in the mirror. Even if I close my eyes to get rid of the image. Instead, the tableau comes alive and the rest of the scene materializes and I see myself still sitting up on the bed in front of the mirror and Michael putting his hands on my shoulders and bringing his head down until his cheek touches mine. I know just what it feels like; he has extraordinarily soft skin for a man and I remember it and then suddenly I'm back on that narrow bed fifteen years ago and the sensation of Michael's flesh, of the shock of the softness under my hands of the skin of his chest and abdomen.

There's Anthony's closet door. Okay, I'm getting up. I've got to open my eyes. I've got to go into the living room. Get up.

*   *   *

She makes Anthony a stiff Bloody Mary and pours herself a glass of wine.

"Wine?" Anthony asks, looking at her drink as she hands him his own.

"I'm trying to drink less," says Casey.

"Good idea," he says.

"Also less goes farther here," says Casey. "Because of all the sun, maybe."

"You look fabulous," says Anthony.

"Really?" says Casey. "I thought I looked strange."

"Strange?" says Anthony. "No, not at all. Or it doesn't show. In fact, it's astonishing how much glamour you can exude even in that getup."

They walk out into the screened-in porch and settle on the deck chairs.

"Sun will set soon," says Casey.

"I'm very interested in your new awareness of natural phenomena," says Anthony. "I've never known you to notice sunsets before."

Casey smiles. "There's not much to do here," she says. "Anyway, it's quite beautiful, isn't it?"

"Very," he says. "But, now, tell me how you feel. You seem much better than when you left New York."

"I'm much better. I feel pretty good."

"You look as if you do," says Anthony.

Casey lights a cigarette. "Do I really seem better to you?" she asks.

"Absolutely," he says. "In fact, rather smashing."

"Oh, that Welsh charm."

"Not at all. Regardless of my nationality, if I weren't a cautious man, I'd be obliged to fall in love with you."

"You're not angry with me for leaving?"

"Certainly not. Do you think I want to be your jailer?"

Casey tilts her head back and closes her eyes. When she opens them again, Anthony is squinting at the sunset.

"The masked man," she says.

"Mm?" he says.

"You are the masked man," she says.

"I can't imagine why you say that," replies Anthony with obvious irony.

Casey laughs. "It's impossible to know when you're saying what you mean," she says.

"And I'm sure you find that reassuring," says Anthony. "Since you yourself always have so much to hide."

*   *   *

I've never felt as safe anywhere as I used to in the recording studio, safe like in a womb, or in a lab. That's in days of Ex-Lovers I'm talking about. Later when I was on my own and in charge, it wasn't so easy, but when we had the band the guys took care of everything. Each one had his spot behind the board, his own swivel chair, and they sat there making a lot of wisecracks, but deadly serious too, like little boys playing. They all had very long hair then, which makes the image, now that I remember it, somewhat comical. Even Smitty had an Afro then, which gave him a terrifying appearance, and was the target of many jokes. Will had like this carefully tended layered hair that came down just to the bottom of his neck, so he could still pass in the straight world, an option he always chose to reserve. Both Nick and Michael had ridiculously long hair, down to below their shoulders. Nick's hair was often dirty. As often as not, he'd come to the studio straight from bed. I knew his routine because I'd seen it sometimes. Nick always slept all day and at six-thirty the call would come from Ken—Ken always called Nick to make sure he'd show up. Nick would swing his legs off the bed, reach for a prerolled joint off the night table, light it, stand up, put on the same T-shirt, chinos, socks and boots he'd left in a heap on the floor the night before, put out the joint and slide it under the shrink wrap of his pack of Pall Malls, walk out the door and hail a cab. When he got to the studio he ate a candy bar and smoked the rest of his joint. There were always bowls of candy bars and other junk lying around. Whereas these days in recording studios there are platters of fruit. Jesus. The rest of us used to eat

132

sandwiches or eggs and bacon out of foil containers that we ordered from some crumb bum deli, and drink about three million cups of coffee and smoke cartons and cartons of Luckies.

If I wasn't singing, I'd pace around or sometimes lie on the couch. I guess in the early days the couch often had girlfriends, until we ruled them out because the amount of drugs consumed there was getting ridiculous and Ken was frantic we'd all get busted. And I didn't like anybody there when I was singing, ogling me through the glass. So usually, it was just us and the engineers. Toward the end, after Nick died and Michael was using heroin on a heavy basis, his man would often come to the studio with him and he'd be sitting on the couch. Michael was so fucked up by then that none of the rest of us could tell him we didn't want that guy around, sitting there all night reading tabloids. Jesus Christ, I hated that fucking creep. I hope he's locked up somewhere.

I don't know. When Michael was using a lot, I could never decide about him. I mean, I'll admit in a way it turned me on, though I would never have admitted it to him. I didn't want him to die, you know, and he was definitely headed for disaster. I guess it was just in the beginning that it seemed sexy to me. Maybe it was just having competition. Junk was much worse competition for me than any of the girls he ever had, that's for sure. Later, when it got really bad, he just became a drag, never showing up when he was supposed to and nodding off while you were talking to him and just only pretending to respond. Sometimes he didn't even pretend. But I've never been able to decide about junkies. Whether they were the purest or the weakest. They were the front line of something, that's for sure.

There was a period when Will was injecting a lot of speed, until cocaine became his drug of choice. Neither Smitty nor Nick would put a needle in their veins. Smitty was into pharmaceuticals, I think. I'm not sure because he was the most discreet about drug habits of any of us. Sometimes we would all smoke marijuana and the studio would seem to become like a submarine.

I had very long hair then too. Down to my waist. When the band conclusively broke up, I cut it off. I was getting too old anyway.

Nick and I had almost the same color hair.

The thing about Nick dying I never realized until now is that it made me scared of Michael in various ways. I mean beyond what happened on Martha's Vineyard. There'd been something so safe about having this relationship with both of them. Michael, in some pique, some argument about something, once accused me of confusing the two of them, but that isn't true, I never confused them at all. But sometimes I'd have this flareup of attraction for one of them, sometimes the other, and the times I liked best was when I was absolutely symmetrically attracted to both of them, so that in a way they canceled each other out. Sometimes I could feel one of them becoming a little too dangerous for me, like it might get out of control, and then I had this thing I could do in my mind, to concentrate on the other more, until the dangerous feeling went away. It was amazing how well it worked. I don't know whether they ever realized that I did that. Sometimes, I wonder about myself, doing that. It may seem a little brutal, I guess. But, I'll tell you something, we couldn't have had a band otherwise. I mean, it would have been too insane. Although, of course, maybe that's just an excuse. But . . . what the hey. I don't know. Anyway, the fact about Michael and Nick was, that maybe for the only time in my life, I had this thing that was exciting but not threatening, and nourishing but not stifling, and just, like, that was completely safe. It wasn't that I confused them, it was that they equalized one another.

When Nicky died Michael became dangerous for me, like a ready and waiting tender trap. I don't know what would have happened if he hadn't picked junk over me. I guess I'll never forgive him for that. Never.

Or would I have just gotten bored anyway?

Maybe I've forgiven him. Maybe there's nothing to forgive.

Maybe it had nothing to do with me. I always think everything revolves around me. Michael used to tell me it was much simpler than it seemed. "You feel bad so you do something about it," he'd say. But I don't know.

What I loved best about the studio is that there are two theaters. There's the show behind the glass, where the recording console is and the show in front of the glass where the performers are. People at the console can talk without being overheard; they have to switch on a microphone to talk to the performers. Though, one night we had an alto sax payer, this guy Red Johnson, putting a solo on a tune and I was out front talking to him after a last take and we had a new engineer who wasn't used to working with us, and he switched the mike on by mistake and I heard Nick say, "Look at this, Casey's got eyes for Red now." And Michael said, "Casey's always had eyes for saxophone players." Which really pissed me off. And Red and I looked at one another for a moment and he smiled at me in a way I liked. The truth is, I always did have eyes for saxophone players, though as a rule I prefer tenor players to alto. They tend to be looser, as human beings. A lot of alto players are control freaks. So I said to him, "Well, in that case, let's split together now," so the guys realized they'd been overheard. They turned off the mike and I saw them looking at one another. "Fuck you!" I yelled to them. Red was standing there holding his horn and looking kind of worried. Michael and Nick behind the glass looked crestfallen. They were a sight.

Actually, I never did split with Red that night. I had a thing at the time for the engineer.

It's really a laugh, but no one ever said no to me. Since my adolescence, not one single man has ever rejected me. Far out, isn't it? I'll tell you something strange, though, in a way it's awful. It's terrible to get to the point where you can have anyone you want. I know it doesn't sound terrible, but it is. Because you just lose all sense of what really is or isn't attractive about yourself. You just become a blur to yourself.

In fact, maybe that's what I like about Anthony. For all that jive British charm, he doesn't bullshit me.

I wish I could stop thinking about Michael.

I wish I could stop this endless teeth-grinding gnashing of

these rotten old memories. There's something about being on this island that's conducive to stepping back into the past. Maybe it's just being with Michael again. Maybe it's all this sunshine and relaxing, my brain easing like a muscle unclenching.

*　　*　　*

For dinner they drive to a restaurant nearby. Casey tells Anthony he'd better start liking fish, and Anthony orders barely cooked tuna and several more Bloody Marys. Casey drinks three glasses of wine, or two more than the quota she'd set herself in the last several weeks.

"This restaurant is an environmental study in obsolete hip," he says.

"Do you find it depressing?" Casey asks.

"No," he says. "I'm quite cheerful."

"I'm really glad you came," she tells him in the car as she steers cautiously toward the house.

"I'm very pleased to be here," says Anthony in his best garden party delivery. "Do you feel okay?"

"Yes," says Casey.

I feel better, she says out loud, half an hour later, in bed. Anthony had gone straight to his own room. *I feel much better.*

When she wakes up the next morning Anthony has come into her bed.

*   *   *

Shit. But it's infinitely too difficult to speak up and ask him to leave my bed. He pushes my hair back and holds my face in his hands the way he always does and I know he's looking at me, but I don't want to open my eyes. I won't open my eyes.

Michael.

*   *   *

After lunch, Michael and Leslie and Anthony and Casey go out to the beach in front of Casey's house. Lulled by lunch and the sun, all four fall silent. Anthony and Michael and Leslie are lying on deck chairs. Casey is lying on her stomach on a towel, letting sand run through her fingers, staring at the ocean. Sometimes Casey turns around and looks at the others. Anthony's craggy features and dark hair seem oddly out of place on this beach, as does the newspaper on the sand beside him, which he insisted on driving into the airport to purchase this morning. Leslie's hands rest on her now huge abdomen, and a very slight smile picks up the corner of her lips. Michael's foot is tapping to some song only he hears. Every time Casey turns and looks at them, one of them has shifted slightly, like in a freeze frame sequence. Usually, they have their eyes closed, but a moment ago, Casey turned around and Michael had his eyes open and he too was staring at the ocean. When he turned his glance met hers.

The ocean today is at its most regal aquamarine, sumptuous and indifferent. The winds are mediocre, and only a few windsurfers dot the waves. The beach, as always, is empty. Beyond the oleander shrubs, the plumeria and the hibiscus hedging either side of the house, there are other houses, but they are too far off for their inhabitants to make their presence felt.

"I think I'll go for a swim," declares Anthony. Casey picks her head up off her arms and sees his shins. She hadn't heard him approach.

"Mm," she hums, and puts her head back down, to preclude

a request to accompany him, but as he walks to the ocean, she picks her head up again and rests her chin on her arm to look at him. Anthony manages not to look ridiculous even at the beach, even though he's both very white and very greasy from suntan lotion.

Casey closes her eyes again, but then reopens them. She turns around. Leslie's eyes are still closed. Michael is looking at the ocean, or perhaps now at Anthony in the ocean. Their gazes meet and part.

"Should we have some music?" Casey asks.

"Yes," says Leslie without opening her eyes.

"Absolutely," says Michael.

"Any requests?" asks Casey.

"I brought you a new tape, you know," says Michael.

"You did?" says Casey, excited. "What?"

"Miles Davis in the fifties," says Michael.

"Oh, that's great," says Casey.

"He spent all yesterday evening and all this morning making the tape," says Leslie. "He even drove into town yesterday because he was missing one album he thought was crucial."

" 'Cookin'?" Casey asks.

"No," says Michael.

" 'Relaxin'?"

"You got it," he says.

"It's really nice," says Casey. "It's really nice of you to do it. I listen to the others all the time."

"I love making these tapes. It gives me the illusion that I'm accomplishing something," says Michael.

"He takes it so seriously," says Leslie.

"Well," says Michael, "the whole point of having a job is to take it seriously."

Casey raises her head and leans on her elbows, "I feel like I never had a job. It seems so long ago already."

"You are telling me," says Michael.

"I never did have a job," says Leslie, who is lying flat out with her hands on her enormous belly, "so I don't feel I'm missing anything."

140

Both Michael and Casey laugh. Leslie pushes up her visor and looks at them questioningly.

"You're too pregnant to say things like that and not get a laugh," says Casey.

"It's true," says Michael. "You're now so pregnant you almost can't say anything without it seeming funny."

Leslie rolls her eyes and emits a mock sigh and puts the straw from her juice glass in her mouth, but it's clear she likes the teasing.

Casey sighs too and leans back on her elbows.

"Look at Anthony," says Leslie. "He's made a job of swimming."

Michael and Casey stare for bit.

"What do you mean?" says Casey.

"Well, he's doing laps," says Leslie. "If you watch him for a while you'll see that he turns around at exactly the same point every time. I think he's using the hibiscus as markers."

"That's funny," says Michael. "He's still in a New York mode."

"It's really funny," says Casey. "It surprises me about Anthony."

"Why?" says Michael.

"He makes an art of seeming spontaneous," says Casey. "Or casual, maybe casual is what I mean."

"He's very glamorous," says Leslie.

"Well," says Casey, "he's elegant."

"Well," says Michael, "he's English. Plus he's very tall."

"Do you like Anthony?" asks Casey.

"Yes," says Leslie. "I loved the way he ate his fruit with a knife and fork at lunch."

"Casey's always had splendid boyfriends," says Michael.

Casey smiles.

"Are you jealous?" asks Leslie.

"I used to be," says Michael.

"It's true," says Casey. "I have had some splendid boyfriends, but there's also a long list of mortifying degenerates of one kind or another."

"Well, they were splendid in their own way," says Michael.

Anthony, who's apparently finished the number of laps he assigned himself, wades out of the ocean, toward them.

"It's fantastic," he says.

"Isn't it?" says Leslie. "It looks really delicious today, so glassy."

Casey stands. "I'm going in the house for the cassette recorder," she says. "Anyone want anything besides more juice?"

"I'll go with you," says Michael.

The kitchen seems cool after the beach. Casey's bathing suit is still damp. She stops in the doorway for a moment. Michael, who's walked ahead, looks back at her. She shakes her head, so he raises his eyebrows but then continues on to the sink. At the sink, he turns around again. Neither of them says anything, they just look at one another. Then, Casey walks to the refrigerator and opens the door and stares inside.

"Maybe I should bring something out for dessert," she says. "We could use some dessert."

Michael, at the sink, is throwing water on his face and chest and Casey realizes he hasn't heard her. She waits until he turns the water off, looking at him, now that she has a chance to do so unobserved. He looks up before she expected him to, as he's shutting off the water, still bent over the sink. His face is dripping.

"You really have a great tan," says Casey.

"I hope so," says Michael. "Because that's all I have."

Casey shuts the refrigerator door and looks at Michael, waits until he straightens up. He tears some paper towel off and wipes his face roughly.

"What's the matter today?" she asks.

"What do you mean?" he says.

"Why do you keep making these put-down remarks about yourself?"

Michael laughs. "I always make these remarks," he says.

"No," says Casey. She lifts her head and looks at the ceiling.

"I haven't seen you tilt your head like that in years," says Michael. "It was always one of my favorite gestures of yours."

Casey frowns. "I didn't realize I did that," she says. "But you're changing the subject."

"You have the greatest neck," he says.

"Gee," she says.

Michael leans against the counter next to the sink and crosses his arms.

"I like your bathing suit," Casey says.

"I don't know," he says. "It must be having Anthony here."

"Oh," says Casey, and, to give herself a countenance, opens one of the cupboard doors, starts to pull out glasses.

"About work, I mean," Michael says very hastily. "Anthony reminds me of a certain kind of thing."

This stops Casey. "What do you mean?" she asks.

"Well, it was the conversation at lunch, I suppose. All of these projects Anthony has and the world he comes from in which everyone has projects. It's just that here this very intellectually energetic, very tall and spectacularly good-looking Englishman arrives, and I don't often have occasion to remind myself that I haven't a clue as to what I'm doing with my life."

"Anthony, like all these writers, always has projects and almost none of them ever pans out," says Casey. She comes over to the sink and turns on the water.

"Well, you know what I mean," says Michael.

"Well," says Casey. "Yes." She bends over the sink to pour water on her face, straightens. Michael is inches away. For once, she really looks at him, from up close: she almost always automatically averts her glance when she is near him and had in a way forgotten his precise appearance. This time she doesn't turn away. Michael looks back and smiles, his mouth a little crooked. But then she sees the muscles slightly contracted around his eyes.

"Do you feel bad?" she asks.

"Why?" he says. "Do I look as if I'm suffering?"

Casey's hands twitch, but she leaves them at her side. "Mm," says Michael. He studies Casey's wet face for a moment. He reaches up and tears a piece of paper towel off and applies it to her damp cheek. Casey smiles and looks down while he dries her face. It's very silent in the room, but neither of them starts when they hear the screen door bang, as if they'd been expecting it. Michael wads up the paper towel and very gently dries Casey's forehead and then throws the wad of paper towel in the garbage just as they hear the bathroom door close.

Michael walks away to the other side of the room and riffles through the cassettes, selects one and puts it into the machine. " 'Wooh,' " he sings along with Howling Wolf. " 'I asked her for water, she brought me gasoline.' "

"Would you like me to help you?" Casey asks.

"Help me?" asks Michael.

"In New York, I mean," says Casey. "I know I could help you get work."

"Playing sessions, you mean?" says Michael. "I'm too out of shape."

"Well, it wouldn't take you long," says Casey. "Or you could produce."

"I don't know," he says. Casey waits. "I don't know if it would be such a good idea for me to be in New York again," he says.

"Well," starts Casey, "I mean, it's great here but . . ."

"No," says Michael. "I mean I don't know if I could be in New York and not want to get high."

"Oh," says Casey. "I didn't realize that was still a problem."

"I think it'll always be a problem," says Michael.

"Really?" says Casey.

"No," says Michael. "Maybe not. I haven't even thought about it in quite a while, actually. It's just I got so accustomed to think of it every time I used to wonder how long I should stay on this island and then I got so used to having my thinking about anything I could do short-circuited by that that I stopped even trying to think about it."

"Aren't you going to run out of money?" asks Casey.

"No," says Michael. He laughs. "That's the problem."

They hear the screen door bang again. They remain quiet and

looking at each other for a moment. Then Casey sighs and turns to the refrigerator.

"I guess I'll just bring juice out," she says.

" 'Tell me, baby,' " Michael sings with the tape. " 'When are you coming back home? You know I love you, baby, but you been gone too long.' "

They select more tapes to bring out. On their way back to their spot on the beach they cross Leslie, who's going back into the house to wake Sebastian from a nap. Anthony's fallen asleep, or at least his eyes are closed. Michael lies down again behind Casey and when she closes her eyes, he looks at her.

*   *   *

I can't believe how his face looked when he brought the paper towel up to my cheek, that tenderness and desire; I'm going to just think about that, about the way he looked then, I'm going to think of it over and over and over again until there's no more ocean or sky or beach or house or Anthony and Leslie and Michael.

*   *   *

"I'm going into town," says Michael. "We're out of every-thing."

"Come with us," says Casey. "We're going too."

Casey is driving. " 'My love burns like a fire,' " she sings. " 'Your love burns like a cigarette.' "

"T-Bone Walker?" asks Michael.

"No," says Casey. "B. B. King."

"You're kidding," says Michael.

"Is there a decent place to have lunch in town?" asks Anthony.

*   *   *

Sometimes I ride around at night by myself, switching the brights on and off, so that the trees loom and then recede into darkness, all the windows open so I can smell the ocean and the earth and the mountain winds. I test myself on the curves.

I went through a period with Nick when I wanted dangerous sex. I mean, to have sex in situations where there was a risk of discovery. Not much of a risk but just enough, for a rush. Nick loved it. Though I guess maybe he would have liked anything that turned me on a lot. Once we screwed in a closet off my dressing room. Once in the isolation booth at the studio. Once, on tour, in the hotel room he was sharing with Smitty, we necked on the bed, when we should already have left for the stadium. The car was waiting downstairs. It was nine forty-five, and the first act was probably winding up. All of a sudden, Smitty came out of the bathroom.

"Well," he said. "Howdy."

I pulled my skirt down. Nick rolled over, zipped up his pants, rolled off the bed and headed toward the bathroom.

"No comment," he said, as he closed the door to the bathroom.

"What a naughty girl you are, Casey," said Smitty.

The door to the room opened and it was Michael. He looked at us. I must have been pretty disheveled.

"What's happening?" he asked. "We're all waiting."

"Casey and me, we was pretty tight," said Smitty. "And it wasn't half bad."

"Jesus Christ!" said Michael, and ran his hand through his hair.

"We're coming," I said.

"Where's Nick?" he said.

Then Will poked his head in. "What the fuck is going on?" he said in that exasperated voice of his.

"Not a thing that concerns you, dickhead," said Smitty.

Then Nick came out of the bathroom, holding a lit joint. "Good morning," he said.

"Assholes," growled Will and slammed the door shut.

Nick lifted up both hands, wearing an expression of perfect innocent puzzlement, and we all laughed.

When we finally got on stage, an hour late, the crowd screamed as loud as I'd ever heard it.

On stage, the boys all wore their best poker faces, except for Smitty. Smitty wasn't afraid to show he loved it. Will always tried to make everything he was playing harder than it was. When we got on stage that night, I jumped up and down for the count, one, two, three, four. And then when the tune started I don't know what got into me, but I did a little dance, all for myself, during the introduction. I'd never done that before. At the chorus, I turned toward Nick and Michael, who were singing backup on the same mike, and gave them this big dazzling, goofy smile. Nick smiled back. Michael raised his eyebrows.

I kept the little dance through all that tour. It worked well, but I had to drop it eventually because the kids would yell so hard it eventually became irritating to play the tune.

That sound, how it thrilled me then. I remember the first time an audience screamed when we got off stage, into the dressing rooms, quickly packed our stuff, rushed through the underground labyrinth to the stage door and into the car and drove away, still hearing that sound, as if it was the building screaming. We kept the windows open when we drove off, though it was bitter winter, to hear that sound.

That night, the night of the little dance, it was Michael I made love with later, in the shower, while we were all supposed to be changing to go to dinner. He soaped my makeup off and then kissed me for about twenty minutes.

He came back to my room with me after dinner, but he went

149

right to sleep. I was really pissed off. I was so wired, it was a 30-milligram-Valium night.

Nick used to scream sometimes when he came. Nick's body was so slender, so boyish. I can't imagine what his body would have been like if he'd lived long enough to become a man. If he were alive now, but the age he was when he died, he could be my son.

* * *

When Anthony and Casey are finishing dinner, while Anthony is still drinking his coffee, Casey announces that she's going for a walk.

"I'll read for a while," says Anthony. But then he adds, "I'll wait up for you," in a firm tone. He looks at his watch.

"I think I need a long walk," she says. "And you're probably tired. You should go to sleep if you're sleepy."

Then, without waiting for an answer, she turns and walks out of the kitchen and through the porch and out of the house, letting the screen door slam.

"Fucking screen door," Casey says out loud to no one.

But once out on the beach, she doesn't walk. She sits down on the sand and looks at the ocean for a while, luminous, still very slightly aquamarine even under a dark sky, then she lies down and puts her face in her hands and cries.

"Oh shit," she says in between sobs. "Oh shit."

*   *   *

Well, I don't know how long I've been lying here crying like an idiot, like I hadn't cried in a long, long time. You know, I hate those fucking people who say "Go ahead and cry, you'll feel better." It never makes me feel better. As a matter of fact, once I start crying about any damn thing I suddenly remember all the other things I have to cry about. And tonight I feel like if I start adding up all the things I have to cry about it's going to be Drown in My Own Tears time, just like the song says. Oh, Ray, if only I could sing like you. If only I weren't stuck in my stupid white girl's body, I wouldn't be lying here eating sand and crying the way you do when you feel it's the end of the road which, of course, let's face it, it is for me. I mean, it's the end of some road for me, this island. I wouldn't be here in the first place if I weren't completely fucked, and now I'm making everything even worse.

I can't believe Anthony has turned out to be such a drag. What an idiot I am to have called for him. Fucking bully jerkoff tyrant. I can't stand the sight of him anymore, I can't stand to hear him talk in that fucking civilized accent of his, I can't stand his perfect wardrobe, I can't stand to have him touch me.

Oh, let's face it, it's not Anthony. The real problem is that I'm going crazy because of Michael. I can't believe this has happened to me, I really can't. I thought I was too old for this. Too old to go crazy this way just because I want to get into bed with someone. I can't believe I can't just talk myself out of this. All I can think of is how it would feel to have my face really close to his, to be lying down with him somewhere looking into his eyes with his mouth just a few inches from mine.

I guess I should go back to the house. Anthony's light is still on. The house seems a million miles away. I don't want to go back into the house. I wonder if Anthony is angry. Well, fuck him if he is. I've got to get myself to calm down.

It's totally terrifying out here, actually. Eerie as hell in the dark, with this perfect half-moon lighting just a patch of the sky and the sense of just miles and miles of cold sand rumpled with footsteps and tire tracks, as wrong as somebody else's unmade bed. And then this scary, noise-filled silence, this constant hiss and roar, that would prevent you from hearing anyone approaching. Rapists, stranglers, men with knives and violent grins, mean hoods, vandals, loud scary kids. Have I told you I'm afraid of the dark? That fucking ocean scares the shit out of me in the dark.

When I was little, my parents rented a house for the summer, a house on the beach. I was real little: my father was still alive. One night I woke up and called out and no one answered so I got out of bed and went downstairs looking for them and walked out the open door onto the beach. The air was filled with moonlight, just like tonight, the sea was black and loud. I saw my parents standing near the water, looking out, and I called to them but they couldn't hear me. And I don't know why I didn't walk out to them. I don't know if I thought they wouldn't want me to or if I thought I wasn't allowed. Or maybe I was just frightened, maybe it felt like a dream, their silhouettes on the moon-filled beach. I started crying and I cried myself into such a fit that I started fumbling around and finally fell down and pounded the sand with my fists, just like tonight.

Maybe that's what it is, maybe I'm just lonely. I'm so lonely.

I just want to make love with him once. I just want to fuck him once. Lord just once just once.

Don't tell me I'm going to get off just pressing against this sand. And what if Anthony comes out? Oh and he'd probably dig it, knowing him. And anyway I don't want to think about Anthony anymore. I don't want to think about anything anymore except Michael, is the truth. Lust is a kind of mantra in a way. It really clears out your brain. I don't know, I wish I could stop thinking all together. I wish I could just go over there and call his name and he'd come down to the beach and I could lie against him. I wish I had the guts to do it, just go over there. I don't know. What would he do? What would Leslie say? Maybe Leslie would say nothing. Maybe Leslie gets the whole thing that's going on anyway. Leslie's not stupid. Maybe if I went there and just beckoned he'd come out of the house and come and lie on the beach with me. But maybe he'd say I can't.

It's not as if Michael and I haven't been in some weird scenes together, either, although, oh my God, it seems so long ago.

There's Anthony, standing in front of the house, framed by the lit doorway of the porch. Is he calling me? Too far to hear. He's going to come out here. Oh, Jesus, just leave me alone. Just leave me by myself for a little while. Is he worried or angry? Maybe he's going to come out here with the big kitchen knife and butcher me up. Oh, that's a laugh. If Anthony saw a big butcher knife, he'd write a limerick about it.

I feel like I'm going crazy.

He's going back in. I am really spooked out here. But at least I'm free. A thick cloud is slipping over the moon. It's going to be even darker now. Don't be scared, Casey. Go with this thing.

One night in a motel, I can't remember which city, I got real scared of the dark. I was so scared of the dark that even when I turned the light on, I was still scared, if you know what I mean. It was really late, late enough so that I should have been patient enough to wait for morning, but it was winter, so I knew it would take a really long time for it to get light. So, as was my wont those days, I decided to go into someone else's bed, and picked Nick's who was in the connecting room. This was in a period when the boys were screwing a lot of groupies, but we'd stayed up late by ourselves drinking in the room that night, so I figured it was cool. We'd left the door unlocked. We were still traveling on a pretty low budget and the boys shared rooms. Nick was sharing a room with Michael; but it was really late and I figured everyone would be asleep. So, really quietly, I padded to the door and really quietly opened it. In their room it was even darker than mine because they had the drapes drawn, so I felt my way with my hands to Nick's bed, nearest the window, like

154

a blind person I felt the texture of his hair and his cheekbones to be sure it was him. Then I lifted the covers and put my mouth next to his ear and whispered "Move over," and he shifted a little and I slid in, into the curve of his shoulder with his arm around me and immediately felt much better, and then I heard this little peep on the other side of him and realized there was a girl in there with him. I was so surprised I just lay there for a moment without moving. Then I thought Oh shit, and I started swinging my legs out of the bed to leave, but Nick kept his arm around me and held my arm tight so I didn't get up but lay still, sort of trying to decide what to do. But then I realized there was something wrong, which was that the room was really quiet. I couldn't hear anybody breathing: no one was sleeping in there. Michael wasn't sleeping either. All of a sudden I flashed on the fact that he had a girl in his bed. I got scared then. That was a new kind of dark to be scared of. Which was weird, in a way, because by then I'd gone to bed with so many strangers I would have thought, if I thought about it, that I was no longer scared of sex. I imagined myself jaded. In a way, then, I liked the fear. And maybe I'd gotten hooked on fear, anyway, addicted to that rush on stage. And then Nick leaned over me and kissed me and I felt this incredibly powerful wave of sensation in my belly, and then the fear melted into the welcoming of the fear just like on stage, and then when Nick pulled me on top of him and I just went with it.

That little girl, she never said or asked anything. To this day I don't know if she knew who it was in that bed. She was just arms and legs and moistness and very small, delicate breasts and very long, light-colored hair draped over all three of our bodies.

And after a time, I could hear the girl in the other bed breathing hard and at one point I turned my head. By then my eyes had gotten used to the dark.

Can I come? Maybe I can come if I touch myself.

Michael was looking at me. They were lying on their sides, and her back was to me, and he was looking at me. I could just see his eyes. By then I was so turned on that his face, all the faces in the room had that strange beauty of that other place where sex

155

happens. Our glances locked and it was, I don't know, so weird. . . . It was eerie like this sea at night. I know he thought so too, because he stopped moving. And then the girl, thinking he was tired maybe, meaning to oblige him in any event, slid down to nestle her face in his groin. My own bed seemed filled with hands, fingers, tongues and I began to swim in that sharp sweet pain of pleasure. There were so many sensations I stopped being able to distinguish among them, though I remember that my lips and the skin inside my mouth were tingling. I knew exactly how Michael felt in that girl's mouth. I mean, I had an exact sense memory of how it had felt to have him in my mouth just a few nights earlier, but I also knew somehow how it felt for him to be in the girl's mouth. Though after a time I couldn't tell whether it was because of someone's mouth on me, was it Nick's or the girl's, or memory or dream. At some point, it must have been the girl's because I just remembered Nick was murmuring in my ear. He was whispering so softly and indistinctly I couldn't really hear him, just felt his lips and breath on my ear. Michael kept looking at me. Sometimes I would close my eyes for a while and then reopen them and he'd still be looking at me. He looked at me until he had to close his eyes.

Do I want to close my eyes now or do I want to come staring up into the sky? I get off on the sky, but I'd rather be with him.

*　　*　　*

When Casey walks back into the house, it's soon after dawn. She gets a glass of juice out of the refrigerator and then sits down on one of the long white couches in the living room, facing the sea. She must sit there holding her glass for quite a long time, for the light is just losing its bluishness when Anthony comes into the living room dressed in the corduroy slacks and the shirt he was wearing the day he arrived.

"Hi," she says.

"Good morning," says Anthony, rolling up his shirt sleeves. She tries to read his face and see if he's angry, but he is studying his sleeve.

"Breakfast?" she says.

"Just tea," he says.

He follows her into the kitchen and sits down while she puts the water on.

"There's a flight at eleven," says Anthony.

Casey turns away from the counter. "A flight?" she repeats.

"Yes, I've booked a seat," he says. "I'm all packed."

"But, Anthony," says Casey vehemently, "I fell asleep on the beach. I was just out there on the beach. I don't know how I even managed to fall asleep out there. But I was by myself."

"My dear Casey," he says. "You know very well that I am the last man who would ever ask you where and with whom you spent the night."

"No, but . . ." starts Casey.

"And it isn't last night, it's within the first few minutes of my arrival here that I began feeling, shall we say, *de trop*."

157

"Anthony . . ." says Casey. The water starts to boil and she turns back to the stove. Anthony watches her for a moment.

"My dear girl," he says. Casey hears the affection in his voice and turns around to look at him.

"It'll be all right." He smiles at her. "Let's have that tea, please."

Casey sets the mug on the table in front of him. "Don't you want anything else?" she asks. "A muffin?"

"No, thank you," he says. "That's been one of the problems, I think. These healthy breakfasts, these walks, these enforced swims, and so forth. It's all putting me off my stride. I'm starting not to recognize myself."

"I know what you mean, in a way," says Casey.

"And there's a tension between us I don't care for."

Casey gets up and goes back to the counter where she begins to fiddle with the coffee things. "I'm sorry," she finally says.

"Oh, it's not your fault," he says, and drains his cup. "There's a little drama going on here that demands your full attention, and my problem is, I don't like to be a supporting player."

"I don't know what's happening here," murmurs Casey.

"No, of course not," says Anthony. "Or you don't think you do. Or you don't want to think you do. That's what makes it a drama. I'll have more tea, if you please."

She brings the pot to the table and sits down. She leans her head on her hand.

"Maybe I should go back with you," she says.

Anthony sips his tea. "Would you like to?" he asks.

"I don't know," she says.

"Perhaps not," he says. She looks at him, rises to pour herself some coffee. "Poor Casey," he says.

She sits down again. "Are you sure you want to go?" she asks.

"You see, supporting players are always fools," says Anthony. "I'm not old enough to play the fool yet. I've got a few years to go on that. But I have to tell you that I'm too old to stay about here, fighting for my territory like some amorous young rooster."

Casey laughs. "You were always too old for that," she says. "Much too suave."

"Nonsense," says Anthony. "You don't know me as well as I thought you did. Or perhaps your understanding of human behavior isn't as sophisticated as I assumed. I don't tend to think of you as naive, but perhaps you're more confused than I thought."

"Don't make me feel bad, Anthony," she whispers.

"Why, darling," he says. He leans toward her and kisses her on the temple. "That is certainly not my intention. Let me give you some advice."

"Yes?" she says.

"Go back to work."

"In New York, you mean? Go back into the studio?"

"It doesn't matter," says Anthony. "Any work. Go back to work."

"I can't," she says. "I don't think I can. That's why I'm here. I don't know how I can go on."

"But that's part of working," he says, "simply to keep going."

"You don't understand," says Casey. "It's very complicated."

"But I do," he says. "I understand precisely. I'm trying to save you months or perhaps years of unhappiness."

"Oh, Jesus," gasps Casey.

"On the other hand," says Anthony, "you may question my motives for giving you this advice. And you'd be right to do so."

Casey lights a cigarette. "Do you want one?" she asks, though she knows he never smokes in the morning.

"Yes," he says. "Absolutely. You know, since I've been here I've had an urge to go back to Pall Malls and drinking whiskey neat." Casey laughs. Anthony lights up, inhales deeply and watches the smoke with telegraphed pleasure. "In fact," he says, "when I see all those lean muscular people on the beach I become conscious of an overwhelming urge to abuse a controlled substance." He smiles at her. "You look marvelous in that yellow," he says. He looks at his watch. "Will you drive me to the airport?"

"Anthony," says Casey. "I really did fall asleep on the beach last night."

"Don't you understand," he says, "that this is a moot point?

159

Surely you don't imagine that I've been haranguing you because I mean to demand fidelity?"

"I don't know what's going on," says Casey.

"Oh yes," he says, rising. "You do."

*　*　*

When I got back from the airport I went into the kitchen to get a glass of juice and put the mugs we had left on the table in the sink. Then I came out here to the beach, since looking at the ocean seems like a logical activity at this point. I don't know. I could go running, I guess. I don't know.

*   *   *

"Yo, Casey!"

Casey starts. She's still sitting on the beach in front of the house, hugging her knees, and doesn't notice Leslie coming up behind her. Leslie's vast now and picks her steps on the sand with much more deliberation.

"Boy," she says to Leslie, "you're just in time."

"Why?" says Leslie, who's reached Casey's spot and is looking out at the ocean.

"For me to make you some lunch, of course," says Casey. She gets up and brushes the sand off her legs. "Are you hungry?"

"I can't tell yet. If you put some food in front of me I'll know."

"Okay," says Casey. "We'll see what tempts you."

"I wish I could have some tapioca pudding," says Leslie as they start walking back to the house.

"Tapioca pudding?"

"Oh, don't pay any attention," says Leslie. "It's just what comes into my mind now that I can't have. I don't know why that's the way my mind works."

"Ain't it the truth," says Casey.

In the kitchen, Leslie finally settles on a bowl of cottage cheese.

"You know, I'm not hungry after all," says Casey. "I think I'll have twenty or thirty more cigarettes for my lunch."

"Has Michael been around today?" Leslie asks.

"Not that I know of," says Casey. "Although I wasn't here. I took Anthony to the airport."

Leslie pauses, a spoon of cottage cheese on the way to her mouth.

"You're kidding," she says.

"No," says Casey.

Leslie brings the spoon to her mouth. "Mm," she says. "This is great cottage cheese. Did you get it at the dairy?"

Casey laughs. "Same old health food store you like. I'm sure they're supplied by tubercular cows."

"You have the greatest smile, Casey," says Leslie.

"And you," says Casey, "are extremely sweet." She brushes her hair back. "I'm really glad you dropped by. I was feeling pretty puny this morning."

"Everybody's in a weird mood today," says Leslie.

"Is Michael in a weird mood?" asks Casey.

"Yeah," says Leslie. "He gets that way sometimes and disappears for a while."

"Anthony had a fit," says Casey.

"Did he?" says Leslie. "I guess it was coming."

"Really?" says Casey.

"Yeah," says Leslie. "Can I have another glass of water?"

Leslie sips her water. Casey lights another cigarette.

"You want to go for a ride?" says Leslie.

"Absolutely," says Casey.

"Have you ever been to Hila Falls?" asks Leslie. "Did Michael ever take you there?"

"No," says Casey.

Leslie slides out and stands. "You'll like it," she says.

The waterfall turns out to be in an exquisite spot in the more dramatic northern end of the island, bounded by weeping willows set in moss. The fall is gentle and where the water gathers in the rock bed, the two women can see schools of small, shiny fish proceeding toward the river in well-organized units.

"Isn't it fantastic?" says Leslie.

"Yes," says Casey. "It truly is. Fantastic is the right word. Like a dream."

"Maybe we are in a dream," says Leslie.

"Definitely," says Casey.

163

"The way the dream ends is that the dreamer has a new dream." Leslie takes off her shorts and her tank top and wades into the stream, just above the fall. Casey sees her tottering on the rocky bottom and calls out, "Are you sure you're okay?"

"I don't know," Leslie calls back. "Maybe this is too tricky for me. I've like totally lost my sense of balance in the last couple of days." She cautiously picks her way back to the bank.

"I miss swimming so much," she says. "I can't even go in the ocean at all. It's really a drag the surf's been so big lately." She sits down on her bundled clothes next to Casey.

"You'd make a great photograph," says Casey.

"Really?" says Leslie, glancing down at herself. "I feel sort of grotesque."

"No," says Casey. "You don't look at all grotesque."

Leslie pats her belly.

"You know what the monkey said when the train ran over his tail," says Casey.

"No, what?" says Leslie, smiling and squinting in the sunshine.

"It won't be long now," says Casey.

Leslie laughs. "Thank God," she says.

"Are you scared?" asks Casey.

"Not too bad," says Leslie. "Sebastian wasn't bad. On the other hand, Frank, Sebastian's father, was with me, and he was really one of these take-charge guys. He really got into it, the breathings, the whole thing. He practically had the baby for me. Michael insists he's going to come to the delivery but I don't know if he can stand it. I hate hospitals. The scariest thing is the hospital, actually. Plus going to the mainland. I mean, timing it right. There's a chopper service that'll pick me up at home and take me directly to the hospital, but I keep thinking of everything that could go wrong."

"What did Sebastian's father do?" asks Casey.

"This and that," says Leslie.

"Ah," says Casey, and Leslie laughs. "And do you still hear from him?"

"Not much," says Leslie. "He and Michael aren't a happening thing."

Now Casey laughs. "I'll bet," she says.

"And he's not comfortable with Sebastian. I think, actually, that's the main reason Michael dislikes Frank is that he's not very nice to Sebastian."

"I'm crazy about Sebastian," says Casey.

"I think you're his first love," says Leslie.

"He does seem to have quite a crush," says Casey. "I'm incredibly flattered."

"Last night he said your name in his sleep."

"Really?" says Casey. "No kidding!"

"You see," says Leslie. "No one can resist you, Casey."

"Oh," says Casey. "I don't know."

"At least no one on Kaulani. Me neither. I think we're all in love with you."

"Well, I'm in love with you too," says Casey.

"But poor Sebastian," says Leslie, "is so in love he's in a state of altered consciousness."

"It's pretty funny," says Casey.

"Which reminds me," says Leslie, and she roots around in the pocket of her shorts, finally extracts a thin joint. "No need to mention this around the house," she says. "Michael thinks I stopped. Have you got a match?"

When Leslie's smoked her joint she leans back against a boulder. "Ah," she says. "That's much better."

"I wish I could get high," says Casey.

"It's really too bad," says Leslie. "But you know, I knew a lot of people who got the willies from grass just because of what they're into at the time and then one day it goes away and they can get high again."

"I don't know," says Casey.

"It's 'cause you've got too much on your mind," says Leslie.

"Well," says Casey. "Yeah, I guess so."

"You should try meditating."

"You're kidding," says Casey.

"No," says Leslie. "I do it. Every morning."

"You do? Really?"

Leslie laughs. "I know it seems corny," she says. "But it really works. Cleans the gunk out of your psyche, you know."

"Yeah," says Casey. "I've got a gunk problem all right."

"Degunks you," says Leslie.

"It would be like marijuana," says Casey. "I can't afford to plumb those recesses."

"That's what Michael says," says Leslie. Casey lights a cigarette. "You and Michael," says Leslie, "say a lot of the same things."

"Yeah," says Casey. "I guess that would figure."

For a while both women look out at the waterfall. Leslie puts her hand on her belly. "You know," she says, "I realize you and Michael have a lot of unfinished business between you."

Casey looks at Leslie for a moment but doesn't say anything. She turns her glance back to the waterfall and takes another drag of her cigarette. Leslie doesn't continue, as if she's waiting for a go-ahead.

"Yeah," Casey says at last. "I guess so."

"Which is sort of tricky to deal with," says Leslie. "I know it makes him unhappy, which I hate to see."

"Seeing me reminds him of a lot of things. Maybe it's bad for him," says Casey.

"No," says Leslie. "I think it shakes him up, though, but that's not necessarily a bad thing."

Casey puts out her cigarette. "Maybe he really should start doing something," she says.

"Work, you mean?"

"Yeah," says Casey.

"That's not what I meant, but that's part of it."

Casey falls silent again.

"We don't have a lot of stupid rules between us," says Leslie.

Casey lights another cigarette.

"I know he'll always be there for me," says Leslie, "at least on some level."

"Yes," says Casey, looking at Leslie again. "I think he will."

"Just like he'll always be there for you."

Casey stands up and brushes the dirt from her backside and her legs. "I'm not really up to this conversation," she says.

"I didn't mean to blow you away or anything," says Leslie.

Casey laughs and sits down again. "What a card you are, Leslie," she says.

"Look," says Leslie, pointing with her chin at the sun glimmering on the waterfall. "Isn't it great? Isn't it just too much?"

"Yeah," says Casey. "It is great." She turns back to Leslie. "I think this baby will be great for Michael," she says. "It'll be great for the two of you to have a child together."

"Yeah," says Leslie. "But you know what?"

"What?" says Casey.

"I slept with other people around the time this baby was made."

Now it's Leslie who keeps her glance on the water.

"You're putting me on," says Casey.

"No," says Leslie. "No, really. Don't tell anybody else, okay?"

Casey looks at Leslie again but Leslie keeps her glance fixed on the waterfall. "I mean," says Leslie, "it's probably not Michael's child."

"Probably not?" repeats Casey.

"No," says Leslie. "Probably not."

Casey waits for Leslie to continue, but she doesn't. "Well," Casey finally says.

Leslie lifts her arms above her head and stretches. "Want to head back?" she asks.

"Does Michael know?" Casey asks.

"Well, I imagine he knows. I mean, he must know. I think he knows."

"Gee," says Casey. But Leslie says nothing more. She stands and flicks twigs and dirt off her legs, so Casey does too.

"It drives me crazy," says Leslie as they walk back to the car. "The bummer part of the whole deal is this has been the best winter for surf we've had in years. It's been one swell after another for two months now. These days are so perfect for being out there with your board."

167

"You miss it?" says Casey. They get into the car.

"Something awful," says Leslie. "But then, I'm really hooked, you know." Casey starts the car. "Let's take the coast road back," says Leslie. "Have you ever driven on it at this end of the island?"

"No," says Casey. They pull out.

"There are some views that'll give you a thrill."

"Good," says Casey. "I could use a thrill."

"Yeah," says Leslie. "Me too."

"Gee," says Casey.

The road emerges cliffside, hundreds of feet above the ocean. Casey stops the car and they look down for a while, silently. Then Casey steps on the gas and they head back.

"I can't believe it," says Casey. "You turn out to be such a bullshit artist."

"Not at all," says Leslie. "What do you mean?"

"You seem so ingenuous."

"But I am."

"You're a really funny girl," says Casey.

"Thank you," says Leslie.

"An incredible bullshit artist," says Casey, shaking her head.

Leslie extracts a roach from her shorts pocket. "Try a little of this?" she asks Casey.

"But what a sweet one," says Casey.

Leslie smiles and lights the roach, holds her breath. "Just an innocent pothead," she expels.

"Yeah," says Casey. "Right."

*　　*　　*

Fucking Leslie! What an outrageous girl little Leslie turns out to be!

And why did she tell me this yesterday? Is she really that generous? Is she much crazier than I thought? Or maybe she was pissed off at Michael. Where was Michael, anyway? Or maybe she really does know exactly what's going on and she's giving me the green light.

Or maybe it means absolutely nothing. Maybe it's true, and she just wanted to tell me.

Maybe she was lying. No. Why would she lie?

Oh, what difference does it make? After all, whether it's Michael's baby or not it's obvious Michael needs Leslie in a certain way, that he's willing to fill a certain slot in that situation. Well, but I do feel it makes a difference.

I wonder if Leslie told Michael that she told me. What in the world is Leslie's take on this? What a tricky girl she is. Of course I'm assuming that she knows everything that's been going on between Michael and me, but that may be ridiculous. I mean, almost all of what has been going on between Michael and me is in my own head. As far as I know even Michael may not know. I mean, I may be in total dreamland here.

No. Oh, I'm really sick of this. This is how God punishes you: by making you waste all this brain time just trying to figure out if your personal scenario matches external reality at all.

Anyway, Leslie may have just been telling me because she needed to tell someone. Or needed to tell me because she thinks of me in a certain way, or wants me to think of her in a certain way.

Well, so then why do I have this deep gut instinct that she told me precisely because it does make a difference and she was giving me a go-ahead?

But why did she never tell me before this?

And I can't believe Michael never told me. How can Michael never have told me?

Though, in fact, now that I think of it, does Michael really know?

Maybe Leslie will have a miscarriage and Michael will be free. No. Don't even let yourself think that.

I haven't even been letting myself think about this baby much; it seemed so clearly to represent and embody all the reasons why Michael would stay with Leslie, which I suppose is the whole point of a baby. But now I don't know what to think about this baby, or about what it is that Michael and Leslie have together. In a weird way, actually, it makes me more shut out than before. I mean, I thought I understood what was between them, and that was bad enough—for me, I mean—but now it seems mysterious and unknown to me in a way it's more painful.

I can just imagine what the white coats would say about that.

Maybe I should call my psychiatrist. No. Fuck that. It's just another way of going nowhere.

And where is Michael today? Maybe something happened to him.

Maybe the phone will ring and it'll be Leslie.

"Michael's real sick," she'll say.

"What's the matter?" I'll ask.

"He's got a very bad fever," she says to me. "I don't know. The flu, maybe. I'm waiting for the doctor, but he lives on the other side of the island."

"Jesus," I say to her.

"He had trouble driving back," she says. "That's why he disappeared today. He went for a drive and was actually not far from where we were but he couldn't get back. He kept having to stop because he didn't see well enough to drive."

"You think it's the flu?"

"I don't know," Leslie says, her voice sounding real small.

Then I'll wonder if he went and got high. "Do you think . . ." I start, but then I pause.

"No," she says. "I mean, I don't know. I don't know what the matter is."

"Can I do anything?"

"Yes," she says. "I was going shopping. The store's going to close and we need some stuff and I want to wait for the doctor. Can you help me out?"

"I'll be right there."

So I'm at the house when the doctor, a very young man with very long hair, wearing a Save the Whales T-shirt, having pronounced that Michael was having some allergic reaction, gives him an injection of antihistamines and another of penicillin and makes him swallow some aspirin for good measure, and then turns to Leslie standing stock-still in the middle of the room, her hand on her belly again.

"Well, so we're a happening thing in this house tonight, right, Leslie?"

Leslie nods.

"When was the last one?"

"Fifteen minutes," says Leslie.

He picks up the phone and calls the helicopter that'll take them to the mainland.

There's only room for one. Scarlet fever. No, malaria. No, snakebite. Snakebite, the long-haired doctor mouths for my benefit only just before closing the door. Half an hour later, the whirring of the helicopter blades recedes and I walk back into the house.

Michael's eyes are open but I can see he's making an effort to focus.

"Goddamn," he says, "I haven't been this stoned in years."

"Well, I wish I was too," I say.

"There's some Robitussin in the medicine cabinet," he says.

It's an old joke between us. I laugh, but Michael's eyes are already closing again.

Is he going to die? Oh my God, oh Jesus. Is that what's going to happen now? And why do I feel this mixture of pain and relief? And this voluptuousness?

At about three, Michael opens his eyes again.

"Hi," I say.

"Hi," says Michael. He lies very still.

"How're you doing?" I say.

Michael seems to think about it but must have forgotten to answer. "Did you talk to him?"

"The doctor?" I say.

"Yeah," says Michael.

"Leslie's okay," I say. "They got to the hospital in time."

"I feel a little crazy," he says. He's having difficulty speaking.

"Well, no wonder," I say. "You got a lot of shit coursing up and down your veins."

He mumbles something.

I'll want to touch him. I'll want to be closer to him. I'll be divided between desire and dread.

"What?" I say. I sit next to him on the bed. I take his hand.

"I'm always a big help, aren't I?" says Michael.

"Yeah," I tell him. "Really."

"I don't know what happened to me," he says.

"You'll be okay," I say.

"I feel like I'm dying," he says.

"Nah," I say.

"I feel like I'm dying of love for you," he says.

Is that what I want to hear from him? Would Nick have said that? Did Nick die of love for me? Or of petulance? Or of the result of having decided he wanted just a little more garbage in his bloodstream? I guess people die of love not for someone else but for themselves. Maybe Michael's not the one I have to get rid of, but Nick, Nick who has been my almost constant companion since he died.

Oh, this solitude is itself a kind of death.

"I'm dying of love for you," says Michael. "Dying of love for you. I'm dying of love for you."

In a way I wish he was dead. I'd rather have him be dead than

172

not love me. Though I guess if someone doesn't love you enough you leave them and then they are dead.

"I'm dying of love for you," says Michael. So close that I can touch him.

I wonder if I'm flipping my lid again. Maybe I should have something to eat.

* * *

Casey hears the door of Michael's car slam shut but doesn't move. She is sitting on the beach again, hugging her knees.

"Hi!" he calls out, walking toward her on the beach.

She waves.

"Not answering the phone?" he asks.

"Hi," she says.

Michael sits down on the sand and looks at her for a moment. "What did you do yesterday?"

"Oh, I don't know," says Casey. "Not much. I guess I was having a prolonged anxiety attack."

"Why didn't you call me?" says Michael.

"You couldn't take it," says Casey.

"Yes I could."

"No you couldn't."

"Are you still depressed?"

"A little better now," says Casey.

"We missed you," says Michael.

Casey looks down. "It was a rough day," she says. "How's Leslie?"

"She's fine. We're getting pretty close."

"Is she okay?"

"Yes," says Michael. "She's fine."

"Where were you the day before?" asks Casey.

"I went for a drive," says Michael. "I was feeling pretty fucked up."

Both of them stare out at the ocean for a bit. "When we go to the mainland, would you like to come with us?"

174

"No," says Casey. "No, thanks. I don't think so."

"Will you be okay here by yourself for a few days?"

"Oh yeah," says Casey. "Fine."

"Well, we can talk about it," says Michael.

"I'll be fine," says Casey.

"I'll call you from there."

"Okay."

"Are you pissed off?" Michael asks.

"No. I guess I'm feeling a little weird."

"Why don't you come back and have lunch with us?"

"No," says Casey. "No, thanks."

"Really? Leslie would like to see you. She's been asking about you."

"No, but say hi to Leslie," says Casey. "I am cooling myself out here. You know?"

"Okay," says Michael, and rises. "Call if you want anything."

*   *   *

Well, it didn't happen like in my fantasy at all. They didn't even need the helicopter. This morning they got on a Lear jet to the mainland, Leslie and Michael and Sebastian. I stood at the gate watching them walk to the plane, a kind of reversal of the day I arrived here, but the same: me by myself and they're a family.

Sebastian cried and cried. As a last resort, he begged to stay with me, but Leslie's mother is waiting in San Francisco.

Poor Sebastian. I wish you didn't have to suffer. I wish this weren't only the beginning.

They should be gone about a week, and I guess that when they come back with the baby, I'll leave. I mean, this is turning into a bad scene. It doesn't matter how generous or loose anybody is, there's a reason why the world is organized a certain way, I guess. The last conversation I had here with Michael was just too weird.

*   *   *

Casey sighs. The moon is rising. "There you are again," Casey says to the moon. "You again."

*   *   *

At the beginning of our first tour I remember we were still wrapped pretty tight. After the shows we used to go back to the hotel and read, for God's sake. I don't know whether we changed because of what we saw while we were on the road or because of what you had to do to your mind to do it, and to go on stage and freak out every night in front of thousands of people, or whether it was just the times. I don't know what would have happened to us if we hadn't had the band. Maybe the boys would have become stockbrokers like everyone else. No, English teachers, maybe. I don't know. On the other hand Will, for instance, came out the other end. He's just what he always was. So did Smitty. But Michael and Nick and I, we got stuck in time, each in our own way. Maybe that's why Nick checked out, really. Maybe in a way the details are insignificant. There was nowhere for him to go from there.

I don't know. All bands fall apart. Just about all of them. They devolve and I suppose their destruction is inherent in the very conflict of personality that gives them vitality in the first place. The good ones, I mean. I keep looking for a turning point, and usually I think it was somehow my fault. I mean, partly because of the weird tensions that were created by my being the only woman, partly because of my fronting the band. But maybe I'm just flying on one of my guilt trips.

On the first tour when we played in little hick towns sometimes the motels didn't even have a restaurant. After the show we'd go to these horrendous all-night places with nightmare fluorescents and worn-out waitresses and eat sickening hamburgers. It was frightening in those places because the locals weren't too fond of boys with long hair. And Smitty, he'd try to make himself real inconspicuous, but you can imagine how easy that was in those days. . . . There was always the danger of needling; maybe violence. We didn't travel with that many roadies then; there were only about ten or twelve of us on any given night, so it was plenty scary. Nick used to call it real life. He used to say it was to remind us why the band had to make it, because a world full of White Castles was waiting for us out there: bad food and tired women and angry men.

Were we happy? It seems to me now, looking back at all our faces around the table, that we were happy, especially in the early days. But of course that's nonsense: we were miserable, or at least thought of ourselves as miserable. We were much too cool to ever act as if we were having a good time. Plus it's true we were really really tired. I guess that image makes me think we were happy because it seems to me like a family sitting around that table. We often squabbled at any given time and two of us would always be agreeing that one of the others was an incredible drag, but in a way that was part of it too, being a kind of family.

It was Will who always took charge. He liked authority and the rest of us didn't. He'd order our food and if necessary dealt with the local toughs. He had this little stock phrase he liked to use. "We don't have a problem with you, so we hope you don't have a problem with us," he'd say, until one night one of those guys stood up and said "You wanna see what a problem looks like?" and walked over with a couple of his pals, slid Will out of the booth and hustled him out of the diner. The rest of us rushed out but were pushed away like little children, with a shove on the chest, while a couple of them beat the shit out of Will.

We went back in and collected Smitty who had prudently stayed inside—he'd warned us from the start that if any trouble ever started he couldn't join in because he would get killed, which was clearly an accurate conjecture—and paid our bill. What good kids we were. Will had nothing broken though he hurt everywhere and his face was like a war map. We went back

179

to the crumb bum hotel and locked ourselves into one room when the roadies left on the truck to take the equipment to the next gig. We spent the rest of the night arguing over strategy to protect ourselves for the rest of the tour. I remember Smitty suggesting we send for a few of his friends from his old neighborhood and Will, lying on a twin bed with washcloths on his face, suddenly wagging his finger no. "More trouble," he had to say several times until we could understand what was coming out of his swollen lips. Nick thought we should hire bodyguards, but after it became clear one of us would have to hit his parents for money, we dropped that option too.

In the end we did nothing. Smoked a joint and left for the airport. Will stopped delivering his little phrase about no problems though, and on that tour we never had any more trouble than being stared at.

When we went out on the road again it was with a much bigger show, playing in bigger towns that had more all-night places, and it was written in our contract that we would have food waiting for us backstage when we were through. Then we began speaking nostalgically of the old days. A year later it was already the old days. Instant nostalgia.

But Will never quite forgave us for not succeeding in rescuing him. "Hey, man, just take a look at me, okay?" Nick would say, opening his arms as if to display his unbelievably feeble 120-pound body. Will and Michael wrote a song called "Don't Let Me Down Again," which wound up becoming a single, which caused us to make jokes about how Will could figure out a way to make money out of anything. It was a pretty good song. A love song, of course. But in fact it was perhaps the first important rift, or at least gave Will a chance to focus his unending free-floating resentment on something, though it mainly took the form of him becoming less willing to share drugs. But pretty soon we all had all the drugs we wanted.

*　　*　　*

The day after Michael and Leslie and Sebastian left the island, it rained. Dressed in shorts and a sweater that was small and badly fitting because it had been left outdoors, Casey sat on her porch and watched the raindrops break the surface of the pool and splatter on the decking around the drenched chaise longues. Toward the end of the afternoon, she put on a plastic poncho and walked out on the beach and stood at the water's edge for a long time. The sea was frothy and restless. Sometimes Casey closed her eyes, as if she was listening. The wind rose and made her shiver. Walking back to the house she noticed the palm trees swaying zanily.

Back inside and dry, she poured some scotch in a glass and sat down and tried to call New York, but the lines were out.

When she turned on the radio, there was a good deal of crackling but she was able to tune in the rock station. She frowned at the sound of heavy metal, but she didn't turn it off. She brought the radio to the porch, and then went back in for her glass, a bottle of scotch, a bowl full of ice. She only got up once, to go to the bathroom and bring back a blanket, with which she covered herself. When she finished the bottle of scotch, she closed her eyes and went to sleep.

In the morning when she woke up she went to the bathroom and then into the kitchen. She couldn't find a serrated knife, so she used her nails, and then, when she failed, her teeth, to tear the plastic seal off the top of a new bottle of scotch. She poured a shot into her juice and took it out to the beach. It was no longer raining but there was an unusual mist hovering over the ocean

181

and the beach. She sat down on the damp sand and didn't move when the wetness permeated her shorts and her underwear. She had almost an entire fresh pack of cigarettes with her and when she rose a couple of hours later, there were eighteen stubs clustered in the sand next to her. She covered up the butts with sand and walked back to the house with her glass. In the kitchen, she put the glass in the sink, got another glass and the bottle of scotch out of the cupboard and went back to the porch, her blanket and the radio. The phone rang and she started but didn't get up. After that when the phone rang she didn't move at all.

The next morning when she got up she went to the bathroom, then into the kitchen where she checked the cupboard to make sure there was no scotch. The sun was out. She changed her sweater to a blouse and drove into town, parked in front of the liquor store, purchased two bottles of scotch, and drove home.

At the beach, she sat in the same place every day. Now she brought the radio to the beach with her though sometimes she turned it off and seemed to listen to the ocean. When she covered that day's collection of butts, she could feel the others under her fingertips.

Two days later, there was no more juice in the refrigerator and no more scotch in the cupboard, but in a corner there was an unopened bottle of local rum and a six-pack of grapefruit juice. That night when she finished the rum on the porch, she didn't go to sleep. She lay for a while in the dark with her eyes open. The radio station went off for the night but it was a few minutes before Casey turned off the radio and the static ended. She lay there for a while with her eyes closed, then opened them again, got up, went to the kitchen, checked to make sure the cupboard was empty and headed for the bathroom just as the phone rang again. She stopped for a moment, stared at the phone and then said "Oh fuck you" out loud.

In the bathroom she opened the medicine cabinet. Not much there: some aspirin, a prescription bottle of Xanax containing five tablets, a prescription bottle of Percodan containing two tablets. When Casey saw there were only two Percodans, she said "Shit" out loud. She held all the pills in her palm for a moment, then closed her fingers on them and walked back to the kitchen just as the phone stopped ringing. "Good," she said.

In the kitchen, she opened her last can of grapefruit juice, poured it in a clean glass and swallowed all the pills at once.

In about twenty minutes she spoke out loud again: "Ah," she said. "Much better."

When she woke up, about sixteen hours later, the sun was already low again. Michael was sitting in a chair next to her chaise longue and when she stirred he turned and smiled at her.

"Hi," she said.

"Hi," he said. "How're you doing?"

"Not bad," she said. "Okay. How's Leslie?"

"Leslie's doing fine," he said. "The baby's great."

"Is it a boy?" asks Casey.

"Yes," he says.

"A little boy," says Casey. "Poor Sebastian."

"What did you take?"

"Mm?"

"I saw the empty bottles in the bathroom," he said.

Casey laughed. "Oh, Michael," she said. "I'm really glad to see you, but you're way off."

He sat back. "You gave me a scare," he said. "It'd been a long time since I got that much of a scare."

"Shit," she said, "people like me don't die."

"Yeah, right," said Michael. "Sure. Tell me about it."

"But you're just in time," said Casey. "I'm just starting to get hungry."

*   *   *

183

part
4

BACK TO THIS. BACK TO ME. YOU KNOW, IF I WAS EVER GOING TO TELL my own story, I'd have to sometimes do it in the first person, sometimes in the third person. Sometimes I just have to dissociate. Usually, I can do it all on my own. But every once in a while some chemical assistance is required. And I have to say that the last few days were a perfect vacation from myself. Phew.

Well, and I can't tell you how much better I feel. I guess I just needed to blitz my brain out of my skull. It's a big risk, of course, this kind of self-help, 'cause you have to figure you may be zapping all kinds of brain cells, and washing the good with the bad down the old biochemical drain, but sometimes it really works out great. Worth the risk. Now everything seems much clearer. I mean, what's clear is how fucked I am, but that's okay. I feel a bit like shit, of course, about Michael leaving Leslie to come here, but what the hell. She's got her mother there. She's all right. Leslie will always be all right. To say nothing of the fact that I'm not displeased to have someone worry about me for once. I also find it pretty darn interesting that out of all the people who were trying to reach me on the phone in those few days and not getting any answer, Michael was the only one who did anything about it. Okay, Anthony, is this a test? Of course my manager was frantic, but that's because he was worried about his accounts for the quarter. Imagine, if I had offed myself, he'd probably have a good few months reissuing some Greatest Hits albums and then he'd have to find himself another turkey.

Or is that what's going to happen anyway? What the fuck am I going to do about my phony-baloney career?

Well, okay, let's take it easy. Let's proceed with care, and take things one by one. First of all, should I go to bed with Michael? I know now he will. I know if I make one move, that's it. He's just waiting for me to make the move, or not make it.

The problem is, I really can't estimate at all what the consequences would be. Maybe nothing. What the hell did Leslie mean anyway in that little chat we had before she left? Was she giving me permission? I don't know. It would seem as though she was, but it doesn't jibe with how people really function. On the other hand, what do I truly know about how people function? Not much, considering the cartoon life I've led all these years.

Well, meanwhile, Leslie has a baby, and I have Michael for a few days.

Do I want Michael to leave Leslie? That's the question, I suppose. Well, no. I don't. I mean, I'd really like a month with him. A month with just him.

Well, it's not a month. Let's just face that. It's a few days. On the other hand, if we make love I don't know what will happen. Sex just throws an element of unpredictability into anything. Which I guess is part of the point of sex, just letting your ego float around the void and watching to see where it alights afterward. Deciding ahead of time what will happen is just bullshit; as soon as you have sex all the givens change.

Oh, I don't know. Maybe that's not true. You lie down, you get laid, you get up, you get dressed, and you go back to your regular life.

I can't stand the responsibility. Fucking someone isn't worth all this responsibility. Oh my God, how old we are. How complicated everything's become.

And, anyway, why is it all up to me? Because he's passive, I guess. Which is why I'd only want a month with him. On the other hand, maybe I'm wrong, maybe Michael knows exactly what he's doing.

No, he doesn't know what he's doing, and neither do I. Neither does Leslie, probably. All of these things only become clear afterward when you can examine your life like a text. While it's happening it almost doesn't matter what you decide, you just have to bulldoze through. So all this rumination, in the end, is just foreplay for smart people.

How could we not make it at this point? It would be ridiculous. Ridiculous.

Well. Ivy divy.

There's a flock of small birds. I never see small birds like that here. Are they going somewhere? Jesus, maybe there are seasons here. I hadn't thought of that. The sea looks kind of agitated today. Maybe there's a storm coming. I could go for a good storm, actually.

No windsurfers. Whitecaps.

That morning on Martha's Vineyard when Michael and Nick and I set out on the beach, there must have been a storm the previous night. Before the sun had a chance to dry it, the sand was packed and damp under our feet. And I remember now there was a streak of green in the gray sea, starting at the horizon, spreading toward us. We stood for a while looking out and I remember trying to estimate what would happen to the weather, which was quite stupid really, since I was the worst kind of city kid and didn't have a clue how to read nature. It made Nick and Michael laugh.

Nick wanted to go for a run. You must be kidding, I said. That was in the days before everyone had a pair of Nikes. In those days we were like devils on stage but spent the rest of our lives in total sedentary indolence. I'm too wasted, Michael said. Nick stood still for a moment. There was a lot of wind whipping our hair around. Then he bolted, like a deer or something, down the beach.

Maybe there were flocks of small birds that day too. Was it fall or early spring? I'm starting to forget. I'm starting to make that day up.

No, not really. I mean, the details don't matter. This isn't made up: the wind and the luminous sky, Nick running, out of sheer exhilaration, barefoot, skinny and fast, getting smaller in the distance, Michael standing next to me looking at Nick, and this electricity between us.

*   *   *

"Hello?"

"Hi, Casey."

"Hi."

"What are you doing?"

"I don't know. Just lying here."

"Lying there?"

"Michael, you've only been gone an hour. I haven't had a chance to work myself up to another bender yet."

"Okay," he says.

"For crying out loud," she says, but she's smiling.

"Are you still tired? Did I wake you up?"

"No, I was just daydreaming."

"Oh," he says, and pauses.

"Hello?" she says.

"Do you want to go for a kayak ride?"

"A kayak ride? Isn't it too choppy?" she asks.

"A little," he says. "It'll be bracing."

* * *

I got faked out on the damn kayak ride. When Michael came to pick me up he was nervous and avoiding my glance again, and I could tell the same thing was on his mind as on mine. I wore the shorts I look best in, and I thought, I don't know, I thought maybe we'd stop on one of the little islands or something, but it turned out the wind was too much to put up with and concentrate on anything else at the same time.

I was all ready, too. Now, I don't know. Maybe I'll just stay in this shower forever. I don't know.

*   *   *

"You look great with your hair wet," says Michael.

"Maybe I should start doing something else with my hair," says Casey.

They're both drinking very stiff Bloody Marys, having made some jokes about switching to hard stuff.

"No," says Michael. "Why?"

"What?" says Casey.

"Don't do anything to your hair."

"Well," says Casey. "Maybe I'm too old for all this blond spiky stuff."

"No," says Michael.

"Should I make a fire?" says Casey.

"Yes," he says. "That would be nice."

She crouches in front of the fireplace. "Are you nervous with me?" she asks, her back to him.

"Yes," he says.

"Nothing bad is going to happen," she says. She ignites the newspaper.

"No," he said.

"Michael!" she says. She turns around and looks at him. "You're becoming monosyllabic."

"Come here," he says. She goes and sits down next to him on the couch and he pulls her head toward his shoulder. He puts his fingers in her wet hair.

"I've always loved your hair," he whispers. Her face is in the hollow between his neck and his shoulder. "And the weight of your head." He threads his fingers through her hair and touches her scalp. "And the shape of your skull," he says. Casey sighs and closes her eyes. "Are you better now?" he asks.

"Yes," says Casey, and her lips touch his skin when she speaks.

"I love your eyelids," he says, touching her. "I've dreamed about your closed eyelids."

"You have?" asks Casey.

"You used to close your eyes sometimes when you sang."

"I know," she says. "I never do that anymore."

"Don't lose that. I'd really like you not to lose that."

"What?"

"The power to go to that other place," he says.

Casey sighs again. "I don't know," she mumbles. "I've been having some tough times."

"I know," he says. And something about the way he says that makes Casey start to cry.

*   *   *

And then I fucking went to sleep! I can't believe that instead of making love I cried like an idiot and then went to sleep like a baby. I mean, what is this? Has my life become some kind of joke? I don't know, I just felt so completely soothed with Michael whispering to me and stroking me and I guess I must have wanted to be treated like a child instead of a woman and he either knew that or somehow wandered into my own personal Twilight Zone. I don't know. This is insane. Is this insane or what?

I woke up a couple of times but just for an instant and he was still holding me. I think he was awake. I was too zonked to even say anything. As though I was sleeping off years of fatigue instead of one darn little bender.

He was holding me tight. Now I realize he was holding me very tight. His arms must have hurt.

And now he's gone.

*　　*　　*

Casey gasps.

"Did I scare you?" says Michael.

"Yes," she says, her hand on her chest. "I thought you were gone."

"I was in the bathroom," he says.

"Oh, God," says Casey, and sits back. "You really scared me."

He sits down on the couch again, but doesn't touch her.

"Look," he says. "It's morning."

"Oh yeah," says Casey, without turning her glance away from him.

Michael laughs. "Look," he says, and puts his hands on her head again and turns her head so she can see out the window.

It's truly dazzling. Pale pinks and pastel blues and milky clouds, the sea placid and imperiously still. On the beach, the palms stand stock still.

"There was no storm," said Casey.

"No," he said. "False alarm."

Casey rolls her eyes. "Oh, Jesus," she says.

Michael laughs. He takes her hand. "Look," he says.

"Yes," she says. She looks away.

"I can't afford it," he says. She looks up at him. "I can't afford to make love with you."

She looks down again. "Okay," she says.

"I know it shouldn't be a big deal, but it is."

"Okay," she says.

"Maybe I'm a fool," he says.

"Yes," she says. "You are."

"And I'll regret this."

"Yes," she says. "You will definitely always regret this. I promise."

"I would have last night," he says.

"I can't believe I went to sleep," says Casey.

Michael laughs.

"I can't believe it," says Casey.

"It was fate," says Michael.

"It was fucking fate," says Casey. "It was the half-life of those fucking Percodans and that booze."

"And the wind on the water yesterday."

"That's right," says Casey. "That absurd wind on that silly ocean."

"Don't call the ocean silly," says Michael, "it might punish you."

"I'm punished already. I'm plenty punished," says Casey.

"Okay," says Michael, and stands. "It's time to go for a walk."

"A walk?" says Casey.

"Yes, a walk," he says. "Otherwise if I hang around here we'll start up again."

"Oh, God forbid," says Casey, in her driest voice.

"I'll go home and clean up and come back for you."

"No," says Casey.

"No?" says Michael.

"No, don't leave," says Casey and she looks at him seriously.

"Well, okay," he says. "But I'm pretty grubby." He runs his hand over his face."

"You can shave here," she says. "I have a razor."

"Oh, one of those ridiculous plastic things, I suppose," he says.

"That's right," she says and smiles at him again when she sees he'll stay.

In the bathroom, Casey watches Michael shaving.

*   *   *

Well, and I can't believe how much I love his face, even with my Noxzema shaving cream on it. I can't believe I'm not going to lie in bed naked with him.

And neither of us has even mentioned Leslie's name who I think is coming back tomorrow if I haven't lost track of time but I don't even want to bring it up because I don't want to hear him talking about her.

And I can't reach out and touch him, because I have to play by the rules of his game. It's only fair. I'd never forgive myself, I guess. Or maybe I would. Maybe this is utterly stupid. Maybe he's only waiting for me to touch him. Then he'll have been honorable, and I will have all the responsibility. Is that what he wants?

He looks so studious. As though he's forgotten me.

*   *   *

"It's very difficult," he says, "to do this while you're looking at me."

"Oh," she says. "I thought you were concentrating."

"No," he says. "I mean, I am, but it's very difficult."

"Oh," she says.

"It's a miracle I haven't cut my throat."

"Do you want me to go into the other room?"

"No," he says.

*　　*　　*

Maybe this is what it would be like if we lived together. Maybe we could do the ordinary things of life and I'd feel this great warmth inside of me just because he was there.

* * *

"Do you think this is what it would be like?" asks Michael.

"If we lived together, you mean?" says Casey.

"Yeah," says Michael. "That doing anything at all, even stupid things, would seem worthwhile just because you were there?"

"Yeah," says Casey. "For a while, anyway."

Michael bends over the sink. "Christ," he mutters as he rinses his face. He dries his face with a towel.

Casey says, "Let me see," and touches his cheek.

"Good enough for you?" he asks. He smiles at her.

"Yes," she says, as if dumbfounded, and snatches her fingers away as if she'd been burned, so he stops smiling.

"Okay," he announces. "The walk."

"Okay," she says.

They drive away from the ocean toward the interior of the island. The vegetation becomes denser, the terrain hilly. Casey drives in silence until Michael abruptly says, "Here," where there is a narrow path Casey wouldn't have noticed.

"Time to put on the sneakers," says Michael. He'd made her bring them. "Snakes."

"Snakes!" says Casey. "You didn't tell me that."

"Nothing too big," says Michael. "Are you game?"

"Well," says Casey, "you know me."

Once on the path, it's junglelike. The air is fragrant, heavy and moist with flowers and rot. Unseen birds are raucous. Under their feet, roots crisscross through the moss. The trees almost meet above their heads, so that the path is dark in spots and they sometimes have to walk bent over.

200

"Far out," says Casey, stumbling after Michael.

"I thought you could use something dramatic," says Michael.

"Yeah, really," says Casey.

"Just try to think of New York now," he says.

Casey laughs. "You're right," she says. "It's almost an impossibility."

After about twenty minutes, Casey starts to get winded and when they arrive at a clearing they stop by a little stream. Casey sits down on a rock. Michael lies down next to her, leans on his elbows.

Casey looks around. "This place," she says, "would have been something on LSD."

"Leslie used to do that," says Michael.

"Really?" says Casey, and then they both fall silent.

After a few moments Michael points upward and they look at an eagle overhead. Then they continue to sit very still. When the birds are quiet for a moment, there are mysterious brushing sounds in the foliage.

"Are there really snakes?" asks Casey.

"Actually," he says. "I've never seen any. I've heard there are."

"I had a fantasy you were bitten by a snake."

"Really?" says Michael. "And what happened?"

"I don't know," said Casey. "I was afraid you were going to die."

"No," says Michael. "No such luck."

"What do you mean!" says Casey. "Don't say that."

"I'm feeling a little freaked out." He looks around.

"Me too," says Casey. "It's scary here."

"Yes. Because it's so voluptuous, you mean?"

"Yes," says Casey. "And those trees are so weird-looking."

"Banyans," says Michael.

"Banyans would be a good thing to use in a song," says Casey.

"All I can think about is sex," he says.

"Me too," she says.

"It's driving me crazy," he says.

"I kind of like it," she says, "though I don't know for how long."

"Do you want to go?"

"No," she says. "Not yet."

After a bit, Casey says, "I feel stoned just sitting here."

"Me too," he says. "In fact I think I'm having a major anxiety attack." He sits up and puts his hand on his chest. "My heart is beating like crazy."

Casey looks at him. "You look a little strange," she says. "Kind of pale. Maybe we should go."

"No," he says. "Not yet." He lies back down again.

"All right. You just tell me."

"I wish I could hold your hand." Casey sticks her hand out in front of her and stares at it. "I'm afraid to touch you," he says.

"Well," she says. "It's okay."

"Do you think you could live with me?" he asks.

"Yes," says Casey.

"Maybe you just think that here," he says. "You couldn't stay here."

"We couldn't stay here, you mean."

"No," says Michael. "We couldn't stay here."

"Maybe you would like it again in New York," she says.

"I don't think you would like me in New York," he says.

She looks at him. "What do you mean?" she says.

Micheal's eyes are closed. "You would tire of me quickly," he says.

"Why do you say that?"

"You did before."

"No," says Casey. "That's not true."

"I think it is," he says.

"It was very complicated," says Casey.

Michael sighs, opens his eyes and looks at her. In this light, his eyes seem very dark green. They look at each other for a moment. "I couldn't take it again," he says.

Casey says nothing and continues to look at him.

"Hello?" he says.

"I can't believe how great you look," says Casey.

Michael smiles and puts his head back down on the moss. "Christ," he says.

"I'm sorry," says Casey. "It's distracting here."

202

"True," he says. His eyes are closed again.

"When you look at me, it's distracting," she says.

"Well," he says. "Being here is almost like having sex."

"That's true," she says. "Look."

"What?"

"I can't believe after all these years that your whole baffling, fascinating manner still just hides this ridiculous lack of self-esteem."

"Are you joking?"

"No," she says. "On the contrary. I just decided to become serious."

"I don't know," he says.

"Maybe you don't really want to have a serious conversation," says Casey.

"I don't know," says Michael.

"I mean, I'm not sure I do," says Casey.

They're both sitting up now.

"I feel weird," says Michael.

"I'm sorry," she says.

"You see, this is the problem," he says. "Everything is so upsetting, and then potentially overwhelming. For a few years now I've been able to protect myself. Of course, I protected myself by fleeing, but I thought that was better. That is, it seemed like my only option."

"I'm sorry," says Casey.

"No," he says. "Don't be sorry."

But he looks sad. Casey slides off the rock and sits next to him. She takes his hand. "Don't be sad," she says.

"No, I'm not," he says.

"I'm starting to feel anxious too. How the hell did we get into this?" she says. "What happened to us?"

"It was to avoid talking about sex," he says.

"Yeah, maybe. It would have been a lot more profitable to make love."

"I think you're right. I don't know. You move me too much. I feel paralyzed," he says. "I'm sorry." He pauses. "I'm sorry," he says again.

Casey holds his hand tight. His palm is warm, hers is cool.

"I can't even talk," he says.

"It's okay," she says. She looks around. "It's too violent here."

"Yeah," he says. "I guess so."

"Let's go. Do you want to go back?"

"Yes," he says.

"We'll go back and we'll have a normal dinner and we'll feel much better."

"Okay," he says.

It's Casey who leads the way back to the road. Once they're in the car they roll up the windows.

"Phew," says Casey.

"Safe," says Michael.

"Though from what, I can't tell you," she says.

"From ourselves, of course."

"You're kidding," she says.

"Yes," he says.

Casey lowers the visor and checks out her hair in the mirror. "I look wild," she says. "Well, anyway, you have to have a little freak-out every once in a while."

"I haven't had this bad a panic attack in a really long time," he says. "I thought I was through with those."

"I still get them," she says.

"You do? Often?"

"Fairly often."

"You're tougher than I am," says Michael. "You go on."

"Well, I don't know," she says. "Not really."

"My heart started beating like mad." He puts his hand on his chest.

"Is it better now?"

"Yes," he says.

"Are you starting to feel better now?"

"Yes," he says. "This silence is merciful. Those fucking birds!"

"Yeah," says Casey. "Really." She turns the key in the ignition.

On the way back they become hilarious over some joke neither of them will remember, just as they sometimes used to when they'd taken a lot of drugs and were finally coming down. Michael smokes one of her cigarettes, which he insists makes him feel as high as a kite. To make Casey laugh some more he starts to speak in a high Mighty Mouse voice. At one point, Casey is laughing so hard she has to stop the car.

*   *   *

Am I going to start to hate him? You can't feel this much lust and pity for someone and not start to hate him, can you?

Oh, I once wanted Nick this way, don't think I've forgotten, but I was of an age then when I wanted all boys that way, all the boys I couldn't have. Months before I even met Michael, I'd spotted Nick at the prep school where we were all marooned and I mapped out, detail by laborious detail, the seduction that would yield the prize of that terribly mysterious boy. How I wanted him. How enigmatic he was. I had the skill of a demon then, in enticing these boys. I was always in the right place, in the right posture, almost expressionless myself but then ready at the strategic moment to seem vulnerable enough to catch him off guard. But I wanted him so badly I must have willed him to love me back. That is, my yearning for him made me crazy, I think, gave me the beauty of insanity. It was a power I barely knew how to use then, I was just starting to figure it out. But I never would have broken through to him otherwise. It was the lesson I learned, to be willing to appear to abandon myself. When Nick finally kissed me, in the hall behind the cafeteria, I put my arms around him and felt him tremble. For a long time, he was my most precious conquest. For however long it took me to tire of the too intense expression of his long pent-up emotion.

It had been worth my virginity, I remember thinking the night we split up, the night I went dancing with a group of kids in which I knew Michael would be included.

They were very generous with me. Or weak maybe. To stay my friends, I mean. No, I think they were generous. I guess it depends on whether I betrayed them. But I don't think I betrayed them. I think they knew me. I *think* they knew me. Better than I knew myself, certainly. I don't know.

Oh, and now all those lovely boys are dead, one way or another, all those boys for whom I sang. It was for them I wanted to be wonderful. I wanted to be wonderful. My God I had this rage to be loved back.

I haven't felt this way in a long time. Is this good or bad?

*　　*　　*

"Michael," says Casey. "Listen to me."

They're sitting in the same corny woody restaurant where Casey took Anthony. They're showered and feeling clean and safe. They're sitting next to one another. Their thighs are touching. They mostly haven't been looking at one another.

"I'm listening," says Michael.

"Why don't you come back to New York?"

He looks up from his salad and turns to her.

"Just like that, you mean?" he says.

"Yes," she says. "Just like that. With or without Leslie and the kids. Come back to New York and we'll do something together. Or we won't do anything together, but I'll help you. There are a lot of things you could do. I can help you."

Michael is looking at his salad again. "I know you could help me," he says. "I don't know if I want help."

"What are you talking about?" she asks. "Are you crazy? What universe are you living in? Come on. Shake it. Just shake all that shit off. Just say the word."

"I don't know. I can't make a move like that, just like that. I don't know."

"If I were you, I'd make that move in a flash."

"It's true, you would, Casey. But you've always been much braver than I am."

"That's not true. It's just that everything's become very hard. We all have weird ways of dealing with it. You ran away to this place. I hung in there and got burned out. It winds up being the same thing, just different ways of managing to survive until the next thing comes along."

"No," he says. "It was always different."

"Weren't we together," Casey pleads, "didn't we just . . ."

"Casey," Michael interrupts. "It was your band."

"What do you mean?" says Casey.

"It was your band. It became yours. You had. . . ." he searches for the word. "I don't know what to call it. Talent, maybe, for lack of a better word. Something that shone and . . ."

"This is bullshit," says Casey. "It was my band by default. Because you guys were all too cool to want to want to be out front, because I was the only one willing to make an asshole of myself."

"Well, maybe that's what talent is," says Michael.

"That's too pat," says Casey.

"No, why?" he says.

"Well," she says. "Would you have wanted to front the band?" There's a silence. "Hello?" she says.

"I don't know."

"Oh, come on," she says.

"Actually," says Michael, "I think I did." -

Casey lays down her knife and fork. "You're kidding," she says. She's genuinely surprised.

"I either couldn't admit it to myself, or couldn't go through the power thing it would have required or, I don't know, something like that. But you know, there was a lot of competition among the guys, and in a way your fronting the band made it a draw among us, because you were a girl, so none of us really had to compete and lose. We saved face, in a way. At least for a while. It didn't turn out to be true in the long run, of course."

"I can't believe this," says Casey. "It just doesn't jibe at all with what I remember of it. In fact, all of you made me feel sort of like a jerk for doing it."

"Well," he says. "Partly it was true that we thought that. I mean, in a way we did think that, but it was partly to cover up the other thing, which we didn't really acknowledge to ourselves. Also, it was just for fun, then. It didn't seem that serious. But then ten years later to find yourself a sideman in a rock band you suddenly start thinking, Is this me?"

"Is that why you left?"

"No. I left because I thought I was going to die. I mean, with whatever glimmer I had left of an intelligence I realized I was going to die if I didn't remove myself." Casey stays silent. "In a way," he continues. "I did die."

"That's what I think," she says. "In a way."

"Or at least continued differently reconstituted."

"But, Michael," she said, "you can't just stay on this island forever."

"No," he says. "Maybe not."

The waiter comes and removes their plates. They order more Bloody Marys.

"I can't get too drunk," Michael said. "Leslie and the baby and Sebastian are due back tonight or tomorrow morning."

"They are?" she asks.

"Yes," he says.

Their drinks arrive. Casey tosses her head. "Let's get a little drunk," she says.

"Okay," he says.

She leans her head on her hand. "I'm already a little drunk," she says.

"I am too," he says.

"It's great when you're not drinking all the time, then you can drink a little and get a little looped."

"It's true, getting a little looped is pretty nice. Seems so innocent to use controlled substances for anything but wiping yourself out totally."

"It's strange not to be excessive," she says.

"I've gotten to like it," he says.

"It's easier here," she says.

"Though sometimes I miss it."

"You do?"

"Yes," he says.

"I can't get over it," she says. "I can't believe you would have wanted to be the lead singer."

210

"Well, then, you don't know me."

"Maybe not."

"Or not really. But then, of course, there was your gorgeous voice."

"But it was you and Nick who taught me how to sing. Everything. How to phrase, what notes to bend, where to breathe."

"That's not true, Casey. In fact, you completely taught yourself."

"No, I didn't. I . . ."

"Well, you hadn't listened to as many blues records as we had. And I remember those days when we'd all get high and Nicky and I would play those sides for you and we'd tell you what we liked and you'd imitate it. But it was a game for us and it turned out not to be a game for you. And you had the equipment. And something else, too. Ingredient X. We knew that."

"I loved your voice," says Casey.

"Yeah, well, it was okay," says Michael. He takes a sip of his drink.

"But then you must have hated me."

"No," he says. "Only myself."

"Do you think that was true of Nick?"

Michael sits back. "Yes," he says.

"And Will?" she asks.

"Certainly Will," he says.

"But you guys always acted as if writing the songs was the really cool thing to do anyway. Always acted as if that was the power job."

"Well, that's true, in a way. I mean that's true, and the other thing is true too."

"Well, so the only reason I did it and all of the rest of this happened to me was that you all didn't want to fight among yourselves or risk losing face or some fucking thing like that?"

"No, of course not," says Michael. "These things aren't accidents. I was too afraid, and you weren't. That's part of it, part of what you have to do."

"What do you mean?" she exclaims. "I was scared shitless!"

211

"Yes," he says. "But you used that."

"You all used to laugh at me."

"Yes," he says. "But that was affectionate. And you knew that."

"Yes," she says.

"And, because of what I'm explaining to you, it was partly nervous too. And, besides, we were all more or less, often more, in love with you. You knew that too."

"Well," she says. "I don't know."

"Sure, you did know that. You got off on that, Casey. Which was okay. I mean, it was our gift to you, I guess."

"Wait a minute," she says. "That may be revision of history."

"I remember," he says.

"I remember too," she says. "A gift?"

"Don't you believe that maybe if you make an erotic connection with someone you want to give them the power of knowing that? That that's a gift?"

"Jesus," she says. "I don't know."

"Well, really," he says. "And I'll tell you something. There wouldn't have been a band otherwise. I mean, we would have fooled around for a few months and that would have been it. It was like there were these erotic lines of force all of which one way or the other passed through you or originated in you. That's what pulled the band together."

"I always thought that way about Smitty."

"I don't mean just musically. Although what you're talking about is basically the same thing I'm talking about. We were really in sync. Perfect sync. But a lot of that was because of this erotic force field I'm talking about, that had to do with you, and that's what gave the group its shape and energy and held it together long past the point where the individuals involved were getting anything good out of it. It was quite amazing, really, when I think about it."

"Gee," says Casey. "An erotic force field. And I always felt like such a jerk, except when we were actually playing."

"Well, there you go."

"But there was the money, too. Though I was never sure, actually, whether you really cared much about the money."

"No, I did. Of course I did. Not in the same way as Will, maybe, but I cared. Though of course I got to the point where I knew what I was buying with all that money was suicide."

"Yeah," says Casey. "Well . . ."

"It's unbelievable how much we admired you. God knows I admired you. Every night I'd watch you do the show from the back of the stage, and as the tour went on, toward the end, your costume would get worn and frayed and sort of crappy-looking and I could see that, which the audience couldn't, and how you'd sometimes hold your thumb when you were nervous, and I'd see you sing your heart out, and you'd seem totally involved in your performance, but then during the solo you'd turn around and make a face at a roadie because you weren't getting the right mix from the speakers. And I got pretty tired of some of your jokes too, that I'd hear every night, but still I admired you because you had this power that was alive even in your immediate periphery on stage, this incredible power."

"Well, it's probably just because you wanted to fuck me," says Casey.

"Sure," he says. "Yes. But that's what it is anyway, isn't it?"

"Plus, you got pretty sick of me," she says. "Toward the end, you guys became a real drag on stage."

"No," he says. "But you got to be more and more of a pro, and we became more and more detached."

"Drugs," she said.

"I don't know," he says. "Life."

"What was wrong with writing songs?" she asks. "What's wrong with writing songs? Why is that dishonorable?"

"I wasn't really good enough."

"Bullshit!" she says.

"No," he says.

"You're kidding yourself. Maybe you're still scared."

"Maybe."

"You're so fucked up."

"I know."

"Oh, I don't know," says Casey, "why I'm giving you such a hard time. I don't know. Maybe you're right and it's a kid's

213

game. Toys for kids. Maybe I should quit myself. Maybe I should face facts and get out while I can do it with some grace."

"What are you talking about?" he says. "Of course you have to keep going."

"But doing what?" she says. "I don't know how to do it anymore. I can't do what I used to do."

"Well, you'll figure out something. That's why you came here. To fuel up so you could figure out something."

"That's not true," she says. "I came here because I was burned out and didn't know where to turn next and had to decide whether to cut my losses or not."

"That's not true," he says. "You came here to get better so you can go on."

"And because of you," she says. "You know I came because of you."

"Yes," he says. "I know." He puts his hand on her neck.

"Oh, God," she says. She closes her eyes. "I can't believe how much I want you to touch me."

"I really want you bad now," he says.

She opens her eyes. "Well, of course," she says. "That's because we're in a restaurant and nothing can happen. If we were in bed naked one of us would go to sleep or have a panic attack or lose a contact lens or there'd be a hurricane or something."

Michael puts his mouth on Casey's neck, notwithstanding the waiter clearing away their dishes. When the waiter leaves, Casey turns her face toward him and he kisses her lips. When he puts his tongue in her mouth she moans. She puts her hand between his thighs and feels him hard. He puts his hand on top of hers and pushes it against his groin.

When the waiter comes again, they sit back.

"How can you not want to make love to me?" she whispers.

"Because," he says, and closes his eyes. "Do you really want to know?"

"Of course I want to know," she says.

"Because you'd hurt me. Because as soon as you owned me you'd crush me."

"What are you talking about! You're sick."

"Yeah," he says. "Maybe."

"That's not how things happen in real life," says Casey.

He opens his eyes. "I don't know," he says.

"You need some psychotherapy," says Casey.

"I've had plenty of psychotherapy," says Michael. "That's why I'm here and not in the gutter. But the gutter waits for me."

"Nonsense," says Casey. Michael kisses her again. "You're making love to me now," she says with her mouth next to his. "You think you're not making love to me now? You don't even have to kiss me. You think you're not making love to me just the way you're looking at me?"

"But you don't own me yet," he says.

"Are you sure?" she says. This time her lips are on his neck. "Are you sure you're not already mine?"

When Michael drops Casey off at her house, she says, "Are you going to come back?"

"I don't know. I've got to check things out at home," he says, pretty woodenly.

"Okay," she says. "You know where to find me."

"Kiss me once more," he says.

She closes the door and leans against it, listens to him back out and drive away. She goes into her room but doesn't turn on the light. She lets her clothes fall on the floor and gets into bed. Her eyes stay open, until dawn. The light in front of the house stays on. Except for the ocean, all is quiet. Every once in a while, she lights a cigarette.

*　　*　　*

Well, no storm. I could never get nature to go along with me. No, the storm that's been threatening all week never came at all. And that fucking ocean is lying there like a big still stinky puddle of blue piss just when I wish it were black and wild and the winds howling, and it turns out not to have been either the storm of my lust or the storm of my defeat. Have I ever been so alone? Yes, many times. All the time, I guess.

Leslie and the baby and Sebastian must be back by now. What is Leslie thinking? Did Michael say anything to Leslie?

And the phone ringing all the time. I'm so sick of it. When will you be coming back? When will you be back? We've got the studio. We've got the rhythm section lined up. Fuck, what do I care?

And they've hired this woman to come and live with them to help take care of the baby. So it's not as if things can go back to the way they were before.

Not that they could anyway.

Why didn't he come back? How could he not come back? Did Leslie arrive already? Why hasn't he called me?

Maybe it really is time for me to split. I mean, I can see how this thing is going to spin itself out. And it's not worth it. It's too big a deal. The truth is, as much as I want him, as much as I crave having him to myself now, I know how little time that lasts. I can't do that to him. How long would it last, a few months? A couple of years, maybe. Maybe. And I suppose I can't really do that to myself. I think some part of me would hate him. Maybe I already hate him. Although now I hate him for refusing to relinquish himself to me and later I'd hate him for having done so.

Do I really hate him? I don't know. I guess I could talk myself into anything.

I'm sure I hate this beach and this incessant sunshine. I wish it were violent out. Not long after I first came here there was an electrical storm and I saw a lot of gulls, this incredible number of gulls over the sea. Groups of them swooping in and away as if they were crazed. The storm made them frantic. Or exhilarated, maybe. And the ocean and the wind were furious, the house rattling, the pool furniture strewn on the hedges, and these sheets of rain crashing against the windows. Why not now when I need it? To think, that night I just went to sleep.

I wish I could be terrified instead of exasperated.

They say there are tidal waves here sometimes.

My God, I can't believe this implosion in my chest. The truth is, this is the perfect state in which to write a song, if I could only get myself to concentrate. From here, it's just a small hop to the zone where you can tap into everything in your brain.

Maybe Michael's right and I should just go back to work. I mean, what choice do I have? It's not a choice, really. But, Jesus Christ, this solitude! Well, that's not a choice either, really. I'm going to be solitary no matter what I do or who I do it with. When have I not been solitary?

Which reminds me of Anthony, as long as I'm feeling sorry for myself. And what the hell am I going to do about him? I don't know. I'll go back to him, of course. I could do worse than Anthony. Although I could do better too, and probably will.

I bet he's waiting for me. The funny thing is that he has got my number. Anthony knows me. Anthony may be the one who knows me truly and the amazing thing is that this turns him on. Maybe it's because he's from an old culture, he doesn't need any new myths. Too perverse to need any newfangled fantasies. I hate Anthony. Do I hate Anthony?

No, I've never had any company when I've really needed it. Songs or storms or men, they come and go in the wind.

In the wind.

The thing about the band was, the thing was that it really did seem like it was going to be a family. Permanent company, whenever you needed it. How did we come to have such contempt for one another? Was it my fault?

But whenever I try to go back to a point where everything was okay I always wind up having to go farther back. How far back would I have to go? There was a party the night before we went on that first tour. It was in some crummy hotel in New York that Ken had booked us into to make sure it would be easy to gather us all together early the next morning. We could still get so excited then. We were all totally wired that night. There was no question of sleeping. I can't even remember what drugs I took, there was so much stuff floating around. I was so thrilled I was like a little kid. At about four or five in the morning or something we decided to hit on a stash of cocaine that Will was saving for the trip. Will had had this idea that he would nurse this stash for the duration and of course we did the whole thing in a half hour. And then Georgie the backup singer had a seizure. A little one, but it scared the shit out of us. She had one snort too many and suddenly her chair tipped backward and she was writhing on the floor, her eyeballs rolled back in her head and making a strange "R" sound in the back of her throat, and her skirt around her hips, her legs thrashing. I remember she had on orange tights. Afterward, she refused to go to the hospital. "Hey, I'm cool," she kept saying, and even wanted to do more cocaine. Of course after one of those seizures, a few years later, she went into a coma and then died. But at the time it didn't seem as though the consequences of anything could be really serious. The party continued.

Smitty was great that night. He thought he'd gotten a chance at the big time at last. He still did drugs with us then, and used to cast the most lubricious eye on the backup singers. It was long before it would become clear that a black guy could only go so far in a white band, or in a white rock 'n' roll business for that matter, and that he'd start to feel too separate from us and began not to hang out with us or want to pick up girls and instead he stayed in his room and practiced. I guess he was also the first one who realized the time had come to take it easy with the drugs and he went on this bizarre health kick and ate only nuts and raisins and stuff like that. And of course wound up using all that power and grace playing studio jingle gigs. All those years of work and all that talent to sell Pepsi. "Hey, heavy bread, you know. And that ain't hay, baby," he says to me when I bump into him in recent years. For a while I continued using him in the studio, but he's starting to lose it now. I mean, in a way he plays better than ever, but it's become a little too slick. His whole laid-back thing has become too routine.

Will was trying to score with Georgie. It's interesting, I realize now, when she had the seizure, it turned him on. It didn't occur to me that night because it wasn't clear yet that he would develop this habit of always hitting on the weakest girls around. Pretty, of course, but basically those who'd become his victims, whom he could control totally as his own personal audience. It was Will who kept supplying Georgie with cocaine long after it was clear she'd keep having the seizures. He became worse and worse as time went on. He'd go on these trips to California and not admit he was trying to get some of his own stuff together there, though we knew he'd split as soon as he got some better deal for himself, and each time he'd come back from there he'd be a bigger drag. Poor sweet Georgie. I hope that while he's rotting in Hollywood maybe every once in a while he wakes up in a sweat in the middle of the night and loathes himself. Probably not.

And Ken, that prick. If he'd known what was coming, he would have been licking his chops that night at the thought of how much money and status he was going to squeeze out of us.

I can't even remember everyone there. Paul. There was Paul, the sound guy who wound up in a mental institution. And Eileen, another backup singer, who became a junkie. I don't know what finally happened to her. Nothing good, no doubt. And Lilian, who married a law professor. And the roadies. I really can't remember the roadies' names anymore except for that guy Sylvester who, without asking me, once spent all night driving to New York and back from Detroit to get a coat from my house for me because I was cold and we weren't anywhere where I could find anything decent to wear.

And then we started singing these Motown songs. These old songs—they were already old. Jerry Butler songs, old Curtis Mayfield type of songs. Or songs that groups like the Shangri-las or the Ronettes or the Temptations used to sing. "Mr. Postman," and "My Boyfriend's Back," and "The Way You Do the Things You Do." Songs you could really wail on. "Tracks of My Tears."

We wound up using all those songs to warm up before we'd go on stage. In the dressing room before the show while I finished putting on my makeup we'd use those old tunes to rev ourselves up to go on. About ten minutes before we were on Ken would stick his head in and bark "Get ready!" and we would all kind of go into another gear and the guys would clown around like kids while I felt this ball of thrill and fear inside my body that would explode and fragment into a zillion molecules within seconds of going on stage.

No, it wasn't big business then, let me tell you. It was a hot minute. A truly hot minute.

At one point we had this way of ending the show where everyone would leave the stage except me and Smitty and I sang the end of the last song a cappella. Michael would always come around and watch me end the show from out in the audience. We had all this weird lighting, then, at the end of the show, and Smitty would be unbelievably hot, and if I was feeling turned on I'd really open it up. Sometimes I could see Michael and if it wasn't in one of those increasingly frequent phases when I was pissed off at him for something or other, sometimes I'd sing to him. I could turn myself on incredibly by doing that. For some reason, doing it for one person makes you feel more exposed then for fifty thousand people. I could really get into it, until the point where I'd enter some weird state where he'd merge with the audience and I wanted them all to fuck me. Or to want to fuck me. I don't know: desire and act seemed one.

And come to think of it, maybe it's around then that I started when I went to bed with anyone not being able to get off unless I fantasized about the crowd.

Was it to fuck me or to love me? It doesn't matter, I guess.

I never felt such ecstasy to be naked. Nuder than flesh. Well, and how pale real life or real sex was by comparison.

And that's what I can't have anymore. You can have that when you're eighteen or maybe even twenty-five but after a while you can't have it anymore. Not on that level, not in that blast-yourself-out-of-the-stratosphere rocket of youth and sensuality. You can't get away with it and anyway you don't want to. You don't have the compulsion and craziness you need to do it right, all the way. And, anyway, I guess the times have changed. Corporate rock. There's that. The culture machine. Thanks a lot. And everyone my age has two kids and an office job and consumes culture. And even the kids. I don't know about the kids. They're not like the kids I knew. They're either completely hopeless or else they're so . . . ridiculous. Were we as ridiculous? I don't think so.

Now it's all become so fucking cerebral. Performance artists they have now. Performance artists! And what were we?

Oh, man, I'm so sick of it.

Ah, I wish I were one of those gulls in the storm, free and fierce. I wish I were like the fire, white and burning hot. I wish I were like the ocean, furious and frothy and endlessly inviting. I wish I were a siren at the bottom of the sea. I wish I were thunder and lightning. I wish I were anything but me.

*   *   *

When Casey walks into their kitchen, Leslie stands and opens her arms and the two women hug one another while Sebastian watches, a thumb in his mouth, and Michael turns away.

Casey stands back from Leslie but leaves her hands on her shoulders.

"You look pale but great," she says. "And I can't believe you're not pregnant anymore."

"I know," says Leslie. "I feel like I was pregnant forever and now I'll have to get used to this other body all over again."

"Me, me!" yells Sebastian, and sticks his head between the two women's bodies.

"Hello, my love," says Casey and crouches to let Sebastian hug her. She sits down and helps him hoist himself into her lap.

"He has to go to bed soon," says Michael.

"No!" replies Sebastian with such ferocity that both Casey and Leslie laugh.

"We were just discussing this issue before you walked in," says Leslie. She turns to Michael. "But I think he should be entitled to a few minutes with Casey."

"Five," says Michael to Sebastian in a new, stern voice. "You have exactly five minutes."

"More," said Sebastian. "Fifty."

"We'll see," says Casey. "How's the baby?" she asks Leslie.

"Timothy," says Leslie. "His name is Timothy. He's a pretty cute baby. But he's pretty pissed off, so far."

"At being alive, you mean?" says Casey.

"Aren't we all?" says Michael.

222

Leslie smiles and sighs. "He's only beginning to understand what a good thing he had going for nine months."

"And how do you feel?" Casey asks.

"I have a new boat," says Sebastian. "Do you want to see it?"

"Yes," says Casey, "absolutely."

He slides off her lap and scampers toward his room.

"I don't know," says Leslie. "Weird. Tired. Weird." She blows a stray strand of hair off her forehead. Her pale hair is pulled back in a barrette.

"Where is this cute baby?"

"Asleep for once," says Leslie. "Do you want to see him?"

"Yes," says Casey.

When the two women stand, Michael does too and begins to clear Sebastian's dinner dishes off the kitchen table.

In the baby's room there is a night light on and a fan twirling on the ceiling and the air seems cool and soft. Casey stands at the crib for a long time, looking at the sleeping baby.

"He sure looks like an angel," she whispers.

"Shhh," says Leslie to Sebastian when he walks in with his boat and he tiptoes ostentatiously over to stand next to Casey in front of the crib.

"Shhh," says Sebastian as they walk out of the room and he puts his finger in front of his mouth like Leslie did. "Look, Casey!" he says when they're back in the kitchen again and they sit down. "Look at my boat." Casey turns toward him.

Michael opens his mouth to speak then closes it then opens it again. "Did you have an okay day?" he finally says.

Casey looks at him and smiles. It's the first time they've looked at each other since she arrived. He smiles back at her. "Yes," she says. "I . . ."

"What do you think, Casey?" says Sebastian still holding out his little blue motor boat. "Do you like it?"

"Sebastian!" says Michael, and slams his hand on the table. "You're interrupting."

Both women look at Michael, startled. Sebastian's face implodes. "I wasn't interrupting," he weeps. "You were interrupting."

"It's time to go to bed," says Michael and stands.

"No, no," cries Sebastian and moves from Casey to Leslie for more secure protection.

Leslie strokes his wet face. "It's really late," she says. "If you go to bed now, you'll be up earlier and I'll take you to the beach first thing. Okay?"

"No," says Sebastian, his head hidden in her lap. "You'll be taking care of the baby. You won't go. You're lying."

"I promise," says Leslie. "Have I ever not kept any of my promises? Lena will take care of the baby, and I'll go with you to the beach."

He doesn't answer. "Okay," says Michael and comes and picks up Sebastian, who is whimpering.

"How about stopping in town first and getting you your own boogie board? How about that?" says Leslie, one finger still in Sebastian's fist.

Sebastian looks up at last. "Really?" he says, with such a transparent expression of hope that this time all three adults laugh.

"Yes," says Leslie. "Really. Now give me a kiss."

Michael bends so Sebastian can kiss Leslie. "I want to kiss Casey," says Sebastian. When Sebastian kisses Casey, Michael's face is only inches above his and hers and Casey looks in his eyes but he doesn't look back.

"Good night, Sebastian," says Casey. "Have wonderful dreams."

"Will you come too in the morning?" asks Sebastian.

"Maybe," says Casey.

"You have to come," says Sebastian.

"Maybe I will," says Casey. "I'll try. If I can, I will."

"Good night, good night," yells Sebastian as Michael carries him out of the room.

"Good night," the women chorus back.

When they've left the room, Leslie groans as she expels her breath. "Man," she says, looking at the ceiling. "Tempers are flaring around here."

Casey laughs because of Leslie's exaggerated irritation. "Your baby is beautiful," she says.

"He's not as easy," says Leslie, "as Sebastian was. And this is only the beginning."

As if on cue, the baby starts crying just as Michael's raised voice wafts out from Sebastian's room. "Labor was easy compared to this," says Leslie, rising. "I don't know where Lena is."

When Casey's left alone in the kitchen she looks out toward the sea, but it's gotten too dark to see, especially from this house, high above the ocean.

Then Michael comes back, but he doesn't look at Casey. Instead, he goes to the counter and pours himself some tea.

"Hello," says Casey.

He turns around and shakes his head and then comes to the table and sits down.

"I'm sorry I'm so fucked up," he says, looking down at the table. "Too much on my plate."

"It's okay," says Casey. She studies his face. He looks worn. "Really, it's okay."

He finally looks at her. "I'm glad to see you," he says.

"I'm glad to see you," says Casey.

"Was your day okay?" he asks.

Leslie comes back into the room.

"My God," she says and flops down on a chair and then winces.

"Are you all right?" asks Casey.

"Yes," says Leslie. "Just exhausted. Totally wiped."

"Maybe you should take it easy," says Michael.

"Maybe I'll split, folks," says Casey.

"No," says Leslie. "It's just the opposite. I'd like to get out."

"Do you want to go for a drive?" says Casey.

"Yes," says Leslie. "God, I wish I could go swimming."

"Do you want to go swimming?" says Michael. "It's a great night for a swim."

Leslie looks really upset.

"I'm game. I'd love to go for a swim," says Casey. "I have a suit in the car."

Leslie smiles. "I don't know," she says, "if I can actually go swimming, but I'd love to go to the beach and just listen to the ocean in the dark and just breathe. That would be sensational. And you two can go swimming."

Both Michael and Casey are silent for a beat. "Well, that's okay," says Michael. "We'll go for a walk on the beach."

"No," says Leslie. "Come on. Put on your suit. I'll be upset if I think I'm a drag." She's clearly in earnest.

"Okay," says Casey and stands. "A swim it'll be. We'll have a swim for Leslie."

Leslie's not up to the descent down to the beach in front of their house, so they decide to drive to another beach, about halfway between their two houses. Casey heads toward her own car, declaring her intention to go home afterward.

"Really?" Leslie says. "So early?"

But Michael says nothing.

*   *   *

I have to leave tomorrow. I can't stand this.

*   *   *

"Oh my God," says Leslie. "Finally, I can breathe."

The three of them have been walking on the beach along the water for several minutes, Leslie on the ocean side, the water swishing around her ankles and calves. Michael walks between the two women, his hands in his pockets.

"It's a beautiful night," he says. And all three of them stop and look out at the ocean and into the sky. The night is particularly balmy. The sea and the sky are so dark tonight that the horizon is undistinguishable. The moon is nearly full, but smudged by clouds, giving the sky a strange dull glow.

"It's only too bad you can't see any stars," says Leslie.

"I never know which are which anyway," says Casey.

"I've learned some," says Michael. "But I'm always too distracted on the beach at night by the sound of the ocean."

"Sometimes I don't think to look up," says Casey.

"Oh, it's the best part," says Leslie.

"I don't know," says Michael. "With less visual stimulation I always concentrate on the sound more."

"How can you call the stars less visual stimulation?" says Leslie.

"I think all this stuff works real well together," says Casey. "You know, like a big sound and light show."

"Well, we're accustomed to think it all goes well together, but actually if you take the components apart . . ."

"Michael," warns Leslie. "You're freaking me out."

"Sorry," says Michael. "I got carried away."

"It's true," says Casey. "If we're not careful we'll soon be

228

talking about infinity and life and death and so forth, and we'll all be freaked out."

"I'm always freaked out."

"It's funny," says Casey to Leslie. "I guess now there are three of you."

"What do you mean?" says Leslie.

"Well, having two children is like having three of you."

Leslie laughs. "I don't know if it works that way."

"No wonder you're freaked out," says Casey.

"Casey's always liked three of everything," says Michael.

"I beg your pardon," says Casey. But she's laughing.

"Maybe the clouds will clear," says Leslie, "and we can see some stars."

"Do you want to sit down a little?" says Michael.

"Yes, actually," says Leslie. They settle themselves on the sand a few feet away from the water line. "Well, I'm starting to feel like I'm back in business," she says, and reaches into her back pocket and extracts a joint. "Look at this."

"What?" say both Casey and Michael.

Leslie holds it up and Casey and Michael lean forward to see. "A gargantuan spliff," says Michael.

"That's right," says Leslie. "This is the moment I've been waiting for."

When Leslie lights her joint, her small, delicate face emerges for a moment from the darkness. A little wind blows out one and then another match. On the third, Leslie is seen to be concentrating intensely and Casey laughs again.

"I missed you, Leslie," she says.

"Yeah," says Leslie. "I kind of missed myself." She takes a deep drag. "Ah," she exhales.

"You know what," says Michael. "I think I'll have one toke."

"You're kidding," says Leslie.

"Well, what the hell," he says. "I really could use some alteration of my consciousness, and after all, the worst that will happen is that I'll be up all night in a state of hysterical paranoia. Won't be the first time."

"I don't think one toke can do that," says Casey.

229

"I don't know what you guys get so paranoid about anyway," says Leslie. She takes another drag and passes the joint to Michael. He puffs on it a bit. "Mm," says Leslie. "Reckless."

"It's our advanced age," says Casey. She leans back and lies on the sand.

"What?" says Michael, his lungs still full of smoke.

"She's pulling rank again," says Leslie, and she too lies back on the sand. Michael sits cross-legged, his back to them, looking out at the ocean.

"No, I'm not. I'm not saying superior," says Casey, "just different."

"Oh sure," says Leslie.

"Here," says Michael to Casey and waves the joint just above her face.

"Me?" says Casey. "I haven't smoked for years."

"Try it," says Leslie. "You'll like it."

"Oh gee," says Casey.

"What the hell," says Michael. "What have you got to lose?"

"Is this a dare?" says Casey.

"No," says Michael. "That would be unfair. I know you'll always take any dare."

"I can't believe," says Leslie, "how great the sky looks."

Casey takes a joint from between Michael's fingers and takes a drag. "I can't believe," she says, "the size of this joint."

"It's like a cigar," says Michael. "Leslie was saving up her appetite while she was in the hospital."

"Hey," says Leslie. "I have to celebrate the end of my bondage."

"That's true," says Casey. "Here, Leslie, have some more. Go crazy."

The joint circulates several times until Leslie puts it out and carefully restores it to her pocket. "There's still about a third of it left," she says.

"I don't know if I can have any more," says Michael. His voice is hoarse.

"Is it 1969 yet?" asks Casey.

"Almost," says Michael.

"Here you go," says Leslie. "As usual."

"You don't want to hear anymore about 1969, huh," says Michael. His voice is affectionate.

"Me neither, actually," says Casey. "I'm sorry I brought it up."

"I'm starting to feel truly copacetic," says Leslie. "I'm willing to hear about anything you want to talk about. I can't believe, I absolutely can't believe, how great the sky looks. I love the clouds over the moon. They look like gray lace."

"And they move so slowly," says Casey. "Like schooners in the sky."

"Christ," says Michael. "It's the worst of 1969."

"Hey," says Casey. "You better stop being mean to me."

"Me?" says Michael, echoing Casey's tone when he offered her the joint. Casey laughs.

"I like that," says Leslie. "Schooners in the sky."

"Oh, Jesus, Leslie," says Michael. "She was being ironic."

"Why?" says Leslie.

"Never mind," says Michael. "You would have had to have been there in 1969."

"Well, then," says Leslie. "Fuck you."

"You are a mean bastard, Michael," says Casey.

"Were you mean to Casey while I was gone?" says Leslie.

"Was I mean to you, Casey?" asks Michael. He asks the question seriously.

"No," says Casey in the same tone. "You couldn't be mean. You're never mean."

" 'I wish that for just one time,' " sings Michael in his Bob Dylan voice, " 'You could stand inside my shoes.' "

"He's mean sometimes," says Leslie.

"Hey," says Michael. "Do you mind? I'm too stoned for this conversation."

"I can't believe this marijuana," says Casey.

"Pretty good, huh?" says Leslie.

"Light of Christ marijuana," says Michael.

"So, Leslie," says Casey. "Do you mean to tell me this is the state you're in all the time?"

231

"As often as possible," says Leslie, "once Sebastian goes to sleep. Though now I guess I'm going to have to toe the line for a while because of the baby."

"There's nothing in nature as great as the sound of the ocean," says Michael.

"That's a big statement," says Casey.

"All the layers of wave sounds," says Michael, "over that background of pink noise."

"Pink noise?" says Leslie.

"Like on a synthesizer," says Casey, "you can get white noise or pink noise. I'm not sure what the difference is."

"With white noise," says Michael, "you get all the frequencies, all the hertz from 20 hertz to about 20,000 hertz, which is the highest you can hear, the entire hearing range of frequencies. Pink noise is the lowest-pitched." He makes a whooshing sound.

"Like the sound you hear from a seashell," says Leslie.

"Or a huge crowd of people murmuring," says Casey.

"That's the background noise of the ocean," says Michael. "Then the waves breaking in different places all have their own frequencies and rhythms as they go up and down."

"They sound different as they get closer and the water gets white," says Casey. "They start sizzling."

"Fizzling?" says Leslie.

"No, sizzling," says Michael. "Like bacon."

"Then," says Casey, "the waves breaking even closer, breaking on the shore, as they're about to break the frequency gets higher."

"When they're at the top of the envelope," says Michael. "Just like the visual. When they're at the highest point that's where the highest frequencies are. So what you end up with is a basic background pink noise and then the various envelopes of waves breaking that are different distances from you."

Leslie sits up. "I don't know about this," she says. "I don't know about thinking about things that way."

"Why?" says Casey.

"Because it ruins the magic of it, I think," says Leslie. "All those words are so ugly. Frequencies. Hertz."

"No," says Michael. "You can understand what something is and break it down and still be susceptible to its beauty. Even if there's something ugly about it, that becomes part of its beauty, makes it even more magical."

They're all quiet for a moment.

"I don't know," says Casey. "I'm too wasted to think straight anymore. What are we talking about?"

"And then," says Michael. "There's this time-space thing that can be inferred."

"What?" says Leslie.

"From what I was saying about the ocean. I mean, you have this basic background hum which you can say is like history and then you have all these other events that make up the history, all these various different waves being the various events."

"And who knows," says Casey, "what's below the surface? You're only hearing the surface."

"Below the surface," says Leslie, "there are fishes with giant jaws with lanterns sticking out of their noses."

Casey laughs.

"It's true," says Leslie. "Those are real fishes."

"Of course, you could say all this about music," says Michael.

"But let's not," says Casey.

"I'm wrecked," says Leslie. "Are you?"

"Yes," says Casey.

"Totaled," says Michael.

Then they all fall silent, and listen to the ocean.

*   *   *

I'm starting to come down a little, which is just as well, since I haven't been this high in years. Not bad though. I didn't expect this bliss-out. Still, a bit much. At least I find out if I can feel this good when I'm stoned, I'm not afraid of myself. I think.

I really had forgotten how much I like Leslie. I'm glad Michael and I didn't go to bed. This is better. This is all right. I'm all right. I'm going to be just fine.

And now things are okay between us.

Oh thank God nothing happened. What was wrong with me? Leslie, I think, has nothing else than him. I don't know why I didn't zero in before on how horrible it would have been. It's so clear that her giving me permission, if indeed that was what she was doing, was totally bogus.

And Michael couldn't take it. Not for one minute.

And, actually, I don't know if I could take it. I think it was a fantasy that got me through this stretch. It's not a coincidence that nothing happened.

No, this guilt-lust cocktail is not for me, I don't like this combo. I'm not seventeen anymore, when you can do the grossest thing, and you go, "Oh wow, I can't believe I did that." No, that time's long gone. And somewhere, of course, I know it's what I've been waiting for. I don't know. I mean, you might say that. You're like leading your life more or less, and acting more or less like a regular human being and then for one reason or another you bump into some guy and it makes you have this feeling right in your sugar bowl and when it happens it knocks you for a loop and you think "Ho, what's this, what the hell is

234

going on down there?" like a total idiot each time, as if it's never happened to you before, and the next time you see him you're checking yourself out to see if it happens again and from then on you can abandon all hope for holding on to your regular human hardware. It doesn't matter what the circumstances are, you're steering for the blues, baby, as soon as you get hungry for that particular brand of sweet. If someone comes along who stirs you that way more than once, you're dead. Someone who makes you feel it more than once, you might as well order the coffin for your common sense. Say sayonara to your sanity.

Well, I intend to stay in one piece.

I don't even know why I'm, like, still nursing all of this. Have to let go. I can let go. I can do anything.

Not that I can complain. I've been here three months waiting for what? Surely not some cheap betrayal. But what else could it be? What did I want, a romance? Did I think this was going to be a romance? Well, it needn't have been anything at all, of course. I could have gone back to New York nice and tidy. Or wherever. Or stuck around here and been nice. But then that's not like me, is it? Well, I can let go of this too.

Oh, God, what a beautiful night. Is this peace I feel at last? At least, a pretty good approximation.

Well, I may have to cry uncle and get back to work, but I ain't crying uncle for no man, no sir, I have no intention of resigning myself to anything with any man, ever. Not with Michael, certainly. No, I know in my heart of hearts that Michael can't stand the heat. Can't stand the heat, come to think of it, might be good for some hook line sometime. That's what this will become, some goddamn song. Not even. A line in a song.

Maybe I should go into the ocean. So enticing. So seductive. Like you could melt into it. Drowning fantasies. Merging fantasies. Who needs sex when you have this? So much more erotic than any stupid human act.

Like a crowd.

What was I thinking about?

What I feel now when I look at the ocean, this is what I love best because you can just step over the boundary and lose yourself in it. Then, when you're lost, you no longer need to try to locate yourself.

I wonder if the ocean is a metaphor for a crowd or a crowd is a metaphor for the ocean.

*   *   *

They've been quiet for a long time. Perhaps twenty minutes. The clouds are thicker over the moon, the night is darker. The wind has risen a little and they can also hear it stirring in the leaves of the hala trees and the coconut palms behind them on the beach.

Michael lies back but when he finds himself only inches away from Casey and Leslie on either side of him he sits up again.

"Maybe I'll go into the water," he says. Neither of the women replies. He stands and unbuckles his pants.

"How're you doing?" says Leslie to Casey.

"I don't know," says Casey. "I can't move."

Michael takes off his pants and pulls his T-shirt over his head and walks toward the ocean. Casey sits up. She can see him softly silhouetted against the sky.

*   *   *

When he unzipped his pants I felt a wave of sensation sear between my legs like a whip.

*   *   *

"I would go in if I were you," says Leslie.
"You would?" says Casey.
"You'll be sorry later if you don't."

*   *   *

It's true, it looks too great not to go swimming. I'll calm down if I go swimming.

*   *   *

"Okay," says Casey. "Here I go."

"Okay," says Leslie.

Casey had put her bathing suit on in the car. She lets her shorts drop around her ankles and steps out of them. She stretches then stands still for a moment.

"It's a little scary," she says. "It's so dark."

"That's what makes it cool," says Leslie.

"That's true," says Casey. "Okay, here I go."

"Okay," says Leslie.

Casey walks to the water and lets several waves wash over her feet. The water is very warm. She wades out a bit and then dives in.

*   *   *

Oh my God, this is blissful. Terrifying and blissful.

*   *   *

Casey swims out and after a bit she floats on her back for a while. Then she swims farther out. Now she can see Michael's head and shoulders above the water. She swims over until she reaches him. They're out where their feet can't touch bottom anymore. He's treading water and looking at the sky.

"Hello," she says.

Michael turns to her. They're close enough so they can see one another. Michael turns his head toward the beach and then Casey does too. The beach is lighter than the sea, but Leslie is just barely visible. They're not sure that shadow is her.

A wave brings them a little closer together. Michael puts his hands on Casey's waist. Casey puts a hand on his shoulder.

*　　*　　*

Wet skin, slightly cool under my fingers. Can Leslie see us?

*　　*　　*

Casey feels Michael's hand brush against her thigh and then he pulls the crotch of her bathing suit aside and then, suddenly, he's inside her.

*   *   *

A little inside me, just the tip of him inside me. Will he stop?
Can Leslie see us?
Don't stop.
Am I talking out loud? Don't stop.

* * *

With the seawater for lubrication it takes him a long time to be all the way inside her but finally he uses his hands to pull her to him. Casey puts her legs around his waist.

*   *   *

I was so surprised at his gesture, when he pulled my bathing suit aside and how quickly he was inside me. It was so abrupt it was almost brutal. At first I kept thinking about that. And then when I put my legs around him we started twirling. I don't know why. Twirling in the water, and the sky twirling overhead, and I felt like my cunt was the center of the universe. In the exact center of the bowl made of ocean and sky and beach I had my legs around him and my arms around him and my face next to his and I could feel all that, his wet skin, and his bones under it, his hips between my thighs and my mouth on his neck and his chest pressed tight against mine, and saw the sky and the clouds over the moon and water black and smooth and glassy around us and the sky and heard the waves, and all of it smelled of salt and brine, and all of it was twirling, the beach and the ocean and the sky kaleidoscoping around us, but at the very center, the epicenter, was him inside of me. Sometimes I kept my mouth pressed against his neck so I wouldn't speak or moan because I couldn't tell how far sound carried and I was wondering whether if Leslie couldn't see then could she hear, and would we be able to neither speak nor moan, and then I listened to the wind and the waves and wondered if it would cover the sound, and then I couldn't hear anything anymore or even feel very much except the very center of myself, or the very center of everything, it didn't matter which anymore, while we twirled together in the black water underneath that faintly glowing sky. Sometimes the wind rose and water would hit us in the face and once I swallowed some water and started coughing but he only held me tighter without stopping. At one point he stopped moving inside me and I felt that part of me was at the center of an infinite vacuum. Then he started moving just a little and I felt radii of sensation from the center of me to the limits of everything. Was it only pleasure? It felt like more than pleasure. I still strained to hear: I thought Leslie might call to us. Had we been in the water very long? Would we hear her if she called? How loud were the waves? I couldn't tell anymore whether Leslie would have had to shout or whether we would have heard her normal speaking voice. I pulled my head back to look at Michael but his eyes were closed, and he kept them closed even though he must have felt me looking at him but he pulled me even closer to him so he could get deeper inside me. And then I stopped thinking very clearly, or rather whatever thoughts I had occurred in that zone where you're not sure if your thoughts are your own or the exhalation of some larger entity that you're only a part of, and distinctions you normally make become blurred so that I wouldn't have quite known which were my limbs and which were his and whether he was inside me or me in him, and what was his flesh and what was mine and what was water all around us and in us. And then I think I couldn't hear the sound of the waves anymore, or of the wind in the waves; instead I heard this *silence*. This silence, I remember now being slightly conscious of it, everything had become still, the waves washed over us and each other soundlessly, and the ocean was utterly silent, and it should have occurred to me that this was some aural hallucination caused by sex or something, some nerve endings you need to hear being shut off, but it didn't, I was too far gone. And then I don't know what I thought, or have no words for it, and the only thing that kept me at all connected to the world was a slight fear that I would scream or maybe that I was screaming, that for an instant the universe was screaming all around me and my scream was part of that one, the sound I've always dreamed of.

It was over fast. He arched his back for a moment. Then he swam away from me.

*   *   *

Michael came out of the water first, then, a few minutes later, Casey. When Casey came out of the water, Leslie was standing on the shore looking out at the ocean; behind her Michael had wrapped a towel around himself. The night seemed darker. If Michael or Casey had wanted to study Leslie's expression, they would have had to stand quite close to her, but they didn't; nor did they look at one another. When she had dried her body and her hair with a towel and put her shorts back on, Casey stood, not far from Leslie, and looked out at the ocean for a moment, but if she was trying to note how much could be seen, her scrutiny was too brief to be conclusive. Wordlessly, they walked back to their cars. Casey kissed Leslie's cheek, and Leslie put her arms around Casey for a moment. When Casey turned and kissed Michael's cheek, it was still slightly damp. Then she got into her car and drove home.

When she got home, she poured herself a drink and went and stood on the porch, leaned her forehead against the screen and looked out at the ocean again for a bit. The clouds had not cleared; there were still no stars; but the wind had died and the beach was still and mute. Then she started packing.

*　　*　　*

Man, what a mess. I don't know if I can even say goodbye to Leslie. And Sebastian. Oh, Sebastian, are you saying my name in your sleep? Sebastian, please don't stop loving me when I'm gone.

I know that if I stick around it'll make it easier on Michael and Leslie but I don't know if I can handle it. I can't handle it.

And the hell of it is how much it turned me on. Even now, you know, even now I can replay that little gesture of his when he pulled my bathing suit aside and I'm a lost cause. Even though it's not only not what I wanted, this dirty coupling, it's the opposite of what I wanted.

On the other hand, that may be bullshit.

Man, this guilt thing is too much for me. God, it stings and burns like hell. Yeah, well, I guess it had been quite a while since I'd done anything really bad. My bad quota was at an all-time low. Had to fill my tank. I wonder if he's freaking out now. If I know him, he must be totally flipped out.

I'm too old for this. Was that me? It's funny, because I felt so much inside my own skin for once. Sometimes I'm so far away from myself I feel like I'm watching my life like I'm watching a movie on another planet. Sometimes I'm talking or singing or fucking and I'm really sitting in the back row of the hall, like I got a cheap ticket, bad sightlines, lousy acoustics, I got to crane my neck and strain my ear just to keep track of the show. And sometimes I can't keep track and it goes on without me, it seems like. But in the water back there I was completely me, Casey, yes I know that. No use pretending something got into me. What got

251

into me was me. And that's why if I stick around here I know I'm going to be flat out on my face wondering how long the evening train's been gone. Forget that. I'm moving on.

I still do, actually, I feel totally like myself. It's not pretty. However, I can take this. Sometimes I think I can take anything, that's my problem. Man, but I have got this motherfucking pain in my chest. What is that? Love?

Or shame, maybe. It doesn't matter. All that shit comes from the same place. You think you got that place locked up safe so you won't feel this fucking Roman candle in your chest, you're cool, you're in control, of course you're depressed out of your mind but you're cool, you're wrapped tight, you're okay, and then all of a sudden you take one little false step and you blow the whole thing. Some goddamn man, no less. It's so stupid, so fucking stupid. Some idiot standing there holding a match and it turns out you've got a gas tank between your legs, with a direct pipeline to your heart.

How can anyone have the tiniest little clue of what this raging thing is about? And they have this nice, cute, attractive little label for me: a performer. They don't know anything about what it takes. People call it guts. They think that what it takes is guts. Yeah, well they don't know what that means, guts. A performer. A performer of what? What the fuck do they think it is that I perform? And they talk about something they call talent, as something they call a spark. A spark! They don't know shit about this ball of fire I have to keep hurling away from me that's constantly being reignited inside of me, that the worst violence can't ever extinguish. Nobody does. Nobody at all. You think this is pathology? What is the remedy for being on fire, Doctor? Michael, you tell me, how can I become an extinct volcano like you? How do I do it? Where do I run to? Man, you douse it with alcohol or you hide it somewhere so long you think you've finally lost it and there it is again, just waiting for you.

Yeah, well, depression as asbestos. I don't need any shrink to explain that to me. Is this better? I don't know. It doesn't make any difference.

The hell of it is I know I'll use this. I've used everything else,

I'll use this too, somehow. How often have I dipped into the wound of Nick's death? I've gone to that well over and over again. I've kept it alive for myself, I've saved it and renewed it again and again just to have it to turn myself on with like some sleazebag hoarding a porno magazine to jerk off with.

Why am I so furious at myself? Well, don't you know, I wish I could fuck him all night long. God knows I haven't felt this way for a long time. Thought I was through with that. Thought I just had to work out the practical aspects of making sure that every once in a while that relatively insignificant neurophysiological event would occur and that this was enough. A change of pace from masturbation, every once in a while. Not even as good, but okay for a change of pace. By myself, the crowd is closer, hotter, dirtier, more frightening, the fear indistinguishable from plea-sure. I didn't bargain for this, wanting to be rocked all night long, to fuck him all night long in the water or out of the water, in the sand, in the bed, on the ground, standing up and lying down, all of a sudden craving fuck-till-you're-annihilated sex that makes you forget you can't stand being alive, if you happen to have had the misfortune to remember you're alive. Which is the stupid thing about sex, really, the stupidest thing, is that it both reminds you and makes you want to forget it.

To say nothing of love because, frankly, I can't deal with that at all. No, if I even try to think about that I'll have to take a little trip to the outside of my own skin again and go back to remote-control mode. And I don't think I'll opt for that just now. No, now that I'm here I'll use it for something.

I can't deal with Leslie. He can deal with Leslie. It's his problem. It's her problem. He can deal with himself, I'm not responsible for his pain. It didn't start with me. I mean, don't I have to scrape myself off the floor every day just to make it through the day? Does anyone ever help me? Has anyone ever helped me even once?

My heart. My heart hurts as if it were going to burst. I think I'll leave most of this shit here and send someone to pick it up. I can't stand this anymore. In an hour, I can leave for the airport. Almost weightless, my arms and legs wrapped around him, sometimes I felt like a child being carried. Sometimes I felt as if I was devouring him. I was part of the ocean, he was going to drown in me, I was swallowing him.

Maneater. There's a song title for you. No, it's been done. Jesus, I have the creeps now.

Another dawn.

Fucking ocean. Beautiful and deadly, you took my last bit of decency. I left it there last night. Now you just sit there shimmering and still in the shape of the earth. You win. Everybody loses but you.

Well, I didn't make him make love to me. Nobody forced him.

Oh, that look on his face, I wish I hadn't seen that. I wish I hadn't pitied him so.

Well, he left me once. He'll get over it again. Just left me, for God's sake, on that fucking stage. Grabbed my hair and kissed me and then walked. This time, I'm the one who's going to say goodbye. There, I'm finished with you.

Oh, Lord.

Yeah, well, like Lester Young says, everybody's got them and everybody plays 'em. The blues, I mean. Yessir, I know what's coming now, and let me tell you that I am hightailing it out of here before I get felled. No, not me. I've taken this baby as far as it can go. It's enough being in this goddamn uproar now, all my systems short-circuited like a rocket lost in space. And for what? For a few minutes' worth, for a dirty deed. The hell with that.

Well now, baby, this is what happens when you try to live your fantasies. Always a mistake, except in your songs. Except in your songs, the best affair is the affair you don't have. To tell you the truth, I'm sorry I fucked him.

About the Author

Marcelle Clements is a journalist whose work has appeared in many magazines and the author of *The Dog Is Us*, a collection of pieces. She lives in New York City.